Six Chambers, One Bullet

Simon Quellen Field

To Jenna

Two suitcases lay on the bed, opened and half full. Sandra dumped an armload of jeans and running shoes into one, and glanced at the clock, wiping away tears.

Not enough time.

She rushed into the study to get the laptop computer, glancing at the screen before unplugging it. Scott was still not online. Damn.

Back in the bedroom, she threw the computer on top of the pile of jeans and opened her purse to get her phone. She found Scott's number and selected it, then held the phone to her ear as she walked back into the study and looked around for anything she needed to put into the suitcases. Only what was needed immediately. She could always buy anything she regretted not packing.

Scott's recorded voice joked on the phone, followed by an impersonal tone. She stopped in mid-stride.

"Scott, get out of there right now! He's dead, Scott. They killed him. They'll be coming after you. Just get out, as soon as you get this. Don't use your ID, don't use your credit cards, don't use your own car if you can help it. Don't go anywhere you've ever been before. And don't tell anyone where you are, especially me. And don't — " She stopped, as the impersonal tone sounded again, and the connection clicked dead. She looked at the phone in her hand, then opened the back, and removed the battery. She began to put it back in her purse, but thought better of it, and left it on the nightstand next to the bed. She'd get a pre-paid phone if she needed one.

Another glance at the clock. Fuck it. She closed the suitcases, still only half full each, and carried them to the front door. She opened the door quickly, pulled the suitcases out onto the porch, and locked the door behind her.

She hesitated only for a moment. Scott was in the most danger, since he had done all the dealing with the client. No one would know much about her yet, unless they had been extremely thorough. She would take the chance that they didn't know what car she drove, or where she lived. Yet. But they would find out soon, and she would be far away by then.

She threw the suitcases in the back seat, got in the car, and left, resisting the urge to put her foot all the way to the floor. If someone *were* watching the apartment complex, she would be just another car leaving the parking lot.

I need to make a list, she thought. Prioritize.

First, make sure Scott was all right. He wasn't answering the phone, and he wasn't by a computer, or he'd have seen her email right away. The first didn't mean anything, since he always let the machine answer the phone. But that he wasn't near a computer could mean either he was in trouble or he had figured it out just like she had, and was on his way to nowhere in a hurry, bags half packed, planning his next move on the run.

Second, she'd need money. And a few supplies. Get that done as soon as possible, before they found out where her money was. Banks have employees, and someone like the client would have no problem kidnapping a bank employee or their family to get a trace on her location, or freeze her funds, or simply empty the accounts.

Third, she'd need a new phone. Any drugstore would have one, but she could not afford to stop too close to home. The farther away from where they are looking, the less chance you will be found. She got on the freeway and headed south.

I should randomize the directions, she thought. Flip a coin for left or right, but never head towards home.

Fourth, she needed to get the client caught. She could not run forever. She was in the business of finding people, and she knew that with enough time, she would be found. The client had hired Scott, and people like Scott would hire people like her, and people like her would eventually get the job done. She always had.

She brought up a map on the car's GPS. Looking at the road, she placed her finger on the touch screen, once, twice, three times, at random. *Find a drug store there.*

She pulled off the freeway at the next opportunity and had the GPS find a drug store near the spot she had picked on the map. Fifteen minutes later, she parked the car in the lot and entered the store. Twenty minutes after that, she walked back out with two new Nokia phones and SIM cards for them, paid for anonymously

2

with cash. She also had a Visa Gift Card, paid for with cash. She opened one of the phones and slipped in the SIM card. She got the laptop out of her suitcase and tried to find an open WiFi connection. There were none available from the parking lot, so she drove slowly down the street, checking the display occasionally, until she found one near an apartment building. She pulled into the parking lot of the building and connected to the Internet.

Being in the business of finding people makes you somewhat of a privacy fanatic, but now the stakes were much more serious. She connected to an anonymizing proxy server in Frankfurt before bringing up a web browser and activating the phone using the T-mobile web site.

Now it was time to get far away from this location. She closed her eyes. *The next license plate I see on a car, the last digit means left, if it is even, and right, if it is odd.* The Camry behind her had a plate that ended in 7. She turned right after leaving the parking lot. *Don't be predictable.* She knew she was being much more cautious than she needed to be. But not being cautious enough was not an option. *Make it a habit, so you don't screw up.*

In another half hour, she felt she was far enough away to use the phone. She dialed 911.

"Nine one one emergency," she heard from the little phone.

"Police, please," she said and waited to be connected. The police dispatcher was courteous and brief in her greeting.

"I'd like to report gunshots," she said. She gave the address.

The dispatcher took the information, and there was a brief pause.

"Is there an officer involved?" she asked.

Sandra was surprised. "I don't think so," she said.

"We have officers on the scene," the dispatcher said. "Can you see the squad cars?"

"Um, I left rather quickly," Sandra said.

"Can I get your name and address?" the dispatcher asked.

Sandra hesitated, and then disconnected the phone, and removed the battery. She started the car and got back on the freeway, heading away from home, away from the office, towards the next freeway. She picked a car, and the last digit on the license

3

plate was a 4. She would make a left at the next freeway, which would take her north.

The police were already at Scott's office. Scott had an automatic in his desk drawer. Maybe he had shot the client and was under arrest. She didn't want to think he was dead. In either case, the police would have the emails she had sent, and the phone messages. Unless the client had erased them after killing Scott.

If the police had the messages, they would know she was running from the client. If they did not have the messages, then Scott was dead, and the client would know that she knew who had killed him, and that she was running. But presumably not in her own car, since she had warned Scott against that. But she'd have to get rid of the car soon, anyway. He'd find it missing at her apartment.

She changed freeways and headed north. She needed money. A lot of it. There was no telling how long this would take to play out. And blankets. She had forgotten to bring blankets or towels. She drove for another half hour, and then pulled off the freeway and found a shopping center. She had three ATM cards for different accounts and pulled $500 out of each at the first autoteller she found. When the banks opened in the morning, she would make more substantial withdrawals. Not much was open this late on a Sunday night. She bought some blankets, a sleeping bag, towels, large jugs of bottled water, and a pillow, using her debit card. *Max it out while you can still use it. Then get far away from here in a hurry.*

Back on the freeway, she drove to the next one. Going west would bring her back towards home, so she drove east. A little past midnight, her adrenaline gave out, and she was suddenly tired. She pulled off the freeway at an empty-looking truck stop and filled the tank, paying cash this time. She paid cash at a fast-food place and parked the car in a corner of the nearly empty parking lot, under a tree, away from the cars that probably belonged to the employees, and away from the dumpsters that might get emptied early in the morning.

Once able to relax for a moment, the impact of how her life had just changed took her over. She leaned back in the seat and let

4

the tears fall. Scott might be dead, perhaps her only trusted friend. Any plans she had had for the near future were now also impossible. There was no way she could visit her mother in hospice, or even explain to her sister why she wasn't there. She had been such a private person, only able to make friends across a keyboard except for Scott. She now had no one she could turn to.

Drained, she put together a makeshift bed in the back of the car, and tried to focus on planning her next moves, instead of completely breaking down, but even that was not working. She wanted someone to hold her and tell her everything would be all right, but she was alone and very tired.

§

Sandra slept remarkably well considering the events of the day, and the hard floor of the car with the back seats folded down. The arrival of the garbage trucks and the banging of the dumpsters woke her just as the sun was about to rise. She brushed her hair and took her toothbrush to the restroom of the fast food restaurant, and felt ready to face the day after some coffee and an egg sandwich.

There were no WiFi access points visible on the laptop, so she drove into the small community that surrounded the truck stop until she found one she could use. She moved over to the passenger seat so she could use the laptop without the steering wheel getting in the way.

Scott had not replied to her emails. He knew how to use proxy servers to disguise his location, so he was either dead or in a place where he could not get to a computer, like jail or a hospital.

The emails she did get were routine. A few personal, a few professional. She answered them as if nothing was wrong. Then she set up her vacation responder to tell everyone she was vacationing in Cancun. That would not fool the client, but it might cause him to waste some time checking it out.

She put the battery back in the phone and called Scott's office again. There was no answering machine this time, no joking Scott followed by a beep. The phone just rang and rang. *Something happened to the machine*. It could be full, but that was unlikely. The client may have come by and taken the answering machine. If Scott was already on the run, the messages on the machine might help to find him. Or find others who had figured it out, like Sandra.

She had to use the phone to contact her sister, who read emails once a month at best. She got a machine, which was fine with her.

"Hey sis, I'm going to be out of touch for a while. Business related. If I call, someone might be listening that I want to keep in the dark or mislead. So, if I mention two numbers right at the beginning, and they are both odd numbers, then whatever I say will either be nonsense or fiction. If they are both even, then you can believe what I say. And erase this after you play it. Gotta go."

She dialed the number again. "Me again. I'll be gone for the next 2 to 8 weeks. That's right, 2 to 8 weeks. Tell mom I'll make it down there as soon as I can. Not long, I promise. I'll leave you a number if you need to reach me. This one won't be good for very long."

She sat in the passenger seat, the laptop open, and thought for a while. She'd need an alias, or several. Her savings would not last long. She'd need an income. One that didn't lead back to her. Catherine Wilcox had been able to elude everyone for over a year and still sell her book online. *I can do that.* She had eventually found Ms. Wilcox, of course. Nobody can stay hidden forever. Everyone messes up somewhere. *Learn from the best.*

Wilcox had used a man's name, thinking a technical book would sell better that way. Probably not necessary, but the idea sounded fun, and a little bit of indirection was always nice. A name that was fun to use, that she could remember easily. She discarded several of her first attempts and came up with Xavier Dylan Hargrove. *He'd pronounce it Havie-air, like he was Latin, Havie-air Hargrove.*

She got busy on the laptop. Xavier would need an email account, a Google Voice account so he would have a permanent phone number that could be routed to a disposable cell phone, and a Facebook account to help sell the book. She set him up with a Twitter account and set him up to follow the best people in the computer security business, since he was going to be an expert in that. She set up an automated script so that Xavier would automatically follow anyone who followed him and get lots of followers in a hurry. Mentioning the book on Twitter and Facebook would be free advertizing.

For the book itself she'd dust off some of the lectures she'd given at Stanford. She'd have to re-write them so they would not link Xavier to her, but the research was already done. And there was plenty of new material she could add from her experiences working with Scott. *And from my experiences trying to hide.* That would be an interesting slant. Instead of how to find people, the book could be about how not to be found.

She set up the Google Voice account and entered the number of the disposable phone. She called her sister one more time.

"Me again. It's four minutes to ten. The number you can reach me at is 505 DEDUCES. That's area code 505, 333-8237. Catchy mnemonic, don'tcha think? Belongs to a guy I'm consulting for just for a bit, name's Xavier. He'll get the message to me, just talk to the machine so he can forward it. And send me an email with mom's doctor's number and email address, and the address of the guy from her church who said he'd drop in on her. You know I'm better at those kinds of things if I can do it by email."

Google Voice would send her an email with the voice message as an attachment. That way she could avoid using up minutes on the disposable phone and avoid the risk of the phone being tracked. She could just never put the battery back in. She had tracked Gary Kilmore by sending SMS messages to his phone and reading the location information. If he had only used the phone for short pit stops on the road, she would never have found him that way.

She jumped in her seat when the phone rang and almost dumped the laptop on the floor.

She held the phone to her ear and cheerfully answered, "Hi sis!"

A man's voice answered her greeting, and her stomach tightened.

"This is detective Morgan of the SJPD. Can I assume I have reached Sandra Theresa Millbarque?"

Her heart was beating quickly, and she tried to think. Her first impulse was to hang up and take the battery out of the phone, and then throw it away and get back on the freeway. But if this really was a police detective, he might know something about Scott.

"What's your first name, detective?" she asked. There was a pause at the other end.

"My name is Jack. Jack Morgan."

"Do you have a badge number or something?"

He read her the number.

"I'm going to call the SJPD and have them connect me to you. But not right away. Maybe in half an hour."

"I'll let them know to expect your call," the detective said.

She disconnected and removed the battery from the phone. Back in the driver's seat, she headed back to the freeway. But first she stopped at a convenience store and bought some packing tape, then headed back to the truck stop, smiling at what she was about to do.

She parked close to a big rig next to the restaurant. She put the battery back in the phone and dialed 976 HOT-MAMA. A young woman's voice answered, almost purring her greeting.

"You charge by the minute, right?" she asked the woman on the phone.

"Yes, we do," the woman said, her voice taking on a more businesslike tone.

"Good. Here's what we're going to do. My husband's been calling this number. A lot. And I've had it. I'm going to give you his credit card number, and you're going to keep the line open. Just burn away those minutes. You got that?"

There was a pause. "You want me to just sit here with the phone off the hook?"

"That's right. Go to a movie or something. We're going to max out his card. Are you with me on this?"

"I guess so."

"Good." She pulled out the $25 gift card she'd bought the day before and read off the number, and then confirmed it.

"Bye now, but don't hang up."

"Ok," the woman said, still sounding uncertain.

Sandra got out the packing tape, left the car, and looked around the parking lot. No one was watching, so she reached up under the truck and securely taped the phone to a strut on the undercarriage. *Let them follow this guy all the way to Seattle. Or Los Angeles, whichever way he's going.*

She got back in the car and headed south on the freeway, back the way she'd come the day before. At the next major highway, she turned off and headed east, away from home.

After about 40 minutes, she pulled off into another small community and hunted for a WiFi signal. Parking under a tree for the shade, she got on the Internet using a proxy server in Singapore and looked up the number for the police department back home.

She also ran a search for detective Jack Morgan, using her own search software.

She used the laptop to place the phone call to the police department. Calls using Google were free in the U.S. and required no identification. Xavier Hargrove's email address was already coming in handy.

"Detective Jack Morgan, please," Sandra said to the man who answered the phone.

"Who's calling?" the man asked.

"His bookie," she said. "Or is that nookie? I get those confused."

There was a long pause. "I'll put you through," the man said finally.

The phone rang twice, and then Jack Morgan's voice announced, "This is detective Jack Morgan."

"Who lives at 1306 Morley Street?" Sandra asked.

"1306?" the detective asked.

"That's right," she said.

"That would be my next door neighbor, Mrs. Jensen," Morgan answered.

"And where did you live three years ago?" she continued.

"That would be 1185 Chrissy Road."

"So you really are Jack Morgan," she said.

"And you are Sandra Millbarque," the detective answered.

Chapter 2: He was left hanging, and the suspense was killing him.

The officer at the scene stepped aside so Jack could enter the office. The small room was crowded. Another uniformed officer stood in a corner to allow more room for the group huddling around the body in the chair. One of them was his partner, Jaime Gonzales.

"Took you long enough," Gonzales said, squeezing past an empty ambulance gurney. The medical examiner moved aside to let Jack examine the body.

"Who kills somebody with a piece of wire?" Gonzales asked. He held up the murder weapon. A length of picture hanging wire, with two handles made of wooden dowels.

Jack looked at the wire and then at the bloody marks around the dead man's neck. He felt the arm of the dead man above the elbow.

"Someone pretty strong," he said. "I bet this took a while."

There were evidence cards still standing up around the desk and floor, marking blood splatter. Jack looked around the room.

"Not likely he found that thing in here," he said.

"So, he brought it with him. Premeditated," Gonzales said.

Jack looked over at Gonzales. "If you were planning on killing someone, and you had plenty of time to choose just the right weapon, why not bring a gun, or a knife? Why make it so hard on yourself?"

"You're thinking the guy gets off on it?" Gonzales asked.

Jack shrugged. "Cleaning crew found him like this?"

"No crew, just that one guy. Took one step into the room, saw the dead guy, and stepped back out fast as he could. Took him another 10 minutes to call 911."

Gonzales was holding an evidence bag. He lifted it up. "Dead guy is the owner, Scott Jason Tremain. Does skip tracing, some divorce stuff. Could have had a lot of enemies."

Jack looked at the floor. "How much of this blood was tracked around by our people?"

"None of it," Gonzales said. "Even the cleaning guy knew not to step in it."

"So the doer wiped his shoes off before walking out?"

6

Gonzales looked at the floor. "No footprints. How do you strangle a guy with a piece of wire and not step in the blood?"

"Careful planning," Jack said.

"Like someone for hire?" Gonzales asked, his tone doubtful.

An office called into the room from outside. "Morgan? Dispatch wants to talk to you. They say they have report of shots fired at this location."

Jack took the radio. "I didn't hear anything."

"A call came in just a minute ago," a woman's voice said over the radio. "Same address, said she heard gunfire, called right away. I said we had officers at the scene already, and she hung up."

Jack looked around at the people in the room and those he could see through the door. "Anybody hear shots?" he called out. Heads shook and shoulders shrugged.

"No gunfire here," Jack said into the radio. He handed it back to the officer.

"Related?" Gonzales asked.

"Who knows," Jack said. "A woman. Said she heard shots from this location, just a minute ago. Didn't stay on the line."

As the two of them walked out of the room, Jack motioned to the gurney. "We're done with him. You can take him out."

Jack walked over to the uniformed officer who had let him in.

"Did anything look like it was missing when you got to the scene?" he asked.

"They took a computer, I think," the officer said. "Cables and stuff were on the desk, but nothing was attached. Probably a laptop. Everything was on top of the desk, no keyboard, no mouse. The desk was locked."

Jack turned to Gonzales. "The phone was reading zero messages. Make sure it gets to the lab. See if they can get any deleted messages off of it. I'll have Jules get his phone records. I want to listen to that 911 call. Something's screwy there."

He turned to the officer. "Get me that bag of his effects. I want to open that desk."

The dead man was wheeled out, and Jack went back inside.

7

There was an automatic in the top desk drawer. There was no magazine in it, and no round in the chamber. He found the magazine in the bottom drawer. This was not a guy who thought he would ever have to use the gun.

There was no filing cabinet. There was nothing in the desk that seemed to relate to any business that a private detective might have. It looked like everything was on the missing computer. There was nothing more to go on in the room.

§

   In the morning the next day, Jack listened to the 911 call again. He had called all of the numbers on Tremain's office phone's speed dial, and one of the answering messages sounded like the same voice that placed the call. He had a name and an address, and he had the number the 911 call had been placed from. He looked up at Gonzales, who was chewing on a bagel, cream cheese smeared on his right cheek. Jack made a wiping motion on his corresponding cheek and said aloud, "She's using a burner phone, activated a few minutes before the call. She was nowhere near the scene. Placing a bogus 911 call. She wanted the police to be there, but she didn't know we were there already."
   "If she killed the guy, why call it in?" Gonzales asked.
   "Maybe her lawyer is trying to build a case already, confuse a jury."
   "You gotta low opinion of lawyers," Gonzales answered.
   "My ex-wife is a lawyer," Jack said flatly.
   Gonzales did not reply to that. "Chicks don't kill guys by strangling them with wires," he said.
   "It could have been for hire," Jack answered.
   "When's the last time you worked a murder for hire?" Gonzales asked.
   "Never. You?"
   "Never," Gonzales said. "That's my point. Once in a blue moon stuff. I'm not seeing it."
   "But she knew about it. Before the fact or after. And wanted the police there."
   "If she walked in on him sitting there dead, why not just call 911 from there?"
   "Good question. If she knew it was going to happen, and wanted to stop it, why not just warn the guy?"
   "Good question," Gonzales mimicked.
   "She's not answering at home. What are the odds she's still got the burner phone?" Jack asked.
   "She ditched it right after the call. That's what burner phones are for," Gonzales said.

Jack picked up the phone and held the number up so he could read it. He punched the number into the phone forcefully and deliberately and looked up at Gonzales as it rang.

A cheerful voice answered. "Hi, sis!"

Jack raised his eyebrows at Gonzales, who opened his mouth, pantomiming being dumbstruck.

"This is detective Morgan of the SJPD. Can I assume I have reached Sandra Theresa Millbarque?" Jack said into the phone. He listened to the voice at the other end of the line.

"My name is Jack. Jack Morgan," he said. He listened again. Then he felt for the badge at his belt and read off the number. He listened again, said, "I'll let them know to expect your call," and then turned to look at the receiver after it clicked loudly enough for Gonzales to hear it at the other side of the desk.

"She's calling you back?" Gonzales asked, doubt and sarcasm coloring his tone.

"We'll see," Jack said, and punched four numbers quickly on the phone.

"Jules," he said after a moment. "I need you to get me everything you can on the call I just placed to the following number," he said, reading off the number of the burner phone. "We already have the carrier. I need the location and any other calls made from that phone. Jimmy's got the warrant, or should have it by now. The Tremain thing from last night." He put down the phone.

"You got a warrant already? On what grounds?" Gonzales asked.

"Jimmy got it. Or is getting it. Bogus 911 call. Easy to get after that thing last summer," Jack said.

"You can't hold her on that," Gonzales said.

"Don't need to. Just need to know where she is. She's a person of interest in a homicide, and the warrant will get us the phone records."

Gonzales took his feet off the desk and sat up in his chair. "So now what?" he asked.

10

Jack pulled the computer screen over so that both men could see it, and reached for the mouse. "Now we find out as much as we can about Sandra Theresa Millbarque."

Almost an hour had passed when the phone rang. Jack pushed back the computer monitor, and picked it up on the second ring.

"This is detective Jack Morgan," he said. He paused to listen to the reply.

"1306?" he asked. Another pause.

"That would be my next door neighbor, Mrs. Jensen."

Gonzales raised an eyebrow. Jack gave a thumbs up sign.

"That would be 1185 Chrissy Road," he said into the phone. There was a short pause.

"And you are Sandra Millbarque," he said.

Chapter 3: Because of her, he will be sleeping with the fishes tonight.

Sandra sat in the passenger seat, the computer in her lap, with headphones on her head, speaking into a small, noise-cancelling boom microphone. She ignored the detective's statement of her identity. The call was being recorded, and she might have to go to court with this as evidence.

"Tell me Scott Tremain is OK," she said.

The detective paused on the other end of the line. "I wish I could," he said.

"Do you know where he is?" Sandra asked.

Another pause. "Yes, I do."

"Can I speak to him?" Sandra asked.

This time there was no pause. "Ms. Millbarque, Scott Tremain is deceased. I suspect you knew that."

"Shit," she said aloud. "Then I'm definitely next on his list."

"Next on whose list, Ms. Millbarque?" Morgan asked.

"Cut the Ms. Millbarque shit," she said. "The guy who killed Scott will be after me next. He hired Scott to find William Thomas Johnson. Scott came up dry, so he called me in on it. I do the web work. If someone is using the web, I can find them. I tracked Johnson down using his buying habits. He used to use a Safeway loyalty card to get discounts, and I have a source that can get me the records of what he buys. That lets me build a profile, and I can search for similar purchasing habits in the rest of the database. That gets me a couple dozen targets, and once I can follow someone, I can pin down which one is my guy."

She waited for this to sink in. The detective was slow in putting it together.

"So you found this Johnson guy," he said.

"I didn't know he was in witness protection," Sandra explained. "But my software was still tracking him when he turned up dead, and he was killed while living in a marshal's safe house. So, I do a search on federal witnesses who turned up dead, and I find two more, and each time there was a private detective killed within a week of them finding the witness for someone. That's how he works."

"Why didn't you come to us?" Morgan asked.

12

"Hello? Federal safe house? All three of these guys were being watched by the police when they were killed. The police couldn't keep private investigators from finding them. This guy probably has your phone bugged and key loggers installed on your computers already. I know how people like me find people. I'm not getting near you guys."

There was a pause from the detective. "What can you tell us about the guy who hired you?"

"He hired Scott. He probably didn't know about me until he got to Scott's office. Did you listen to the messages on Scott's phone?"

"There were no messages on the phone," Morgan said.

"Then he knows about me," Sandra said. "I left a ton of messages warning Scott. And emails, since Scott isn't good about checking voice mail. If Scott had gotten any of them, he should have been miles away, or at least armed. But your dispatcher was surprised to learn about gunshots, so I'm guessing he didn't get to use his gun."

The detective asked again. "What can you tell us about this guy?"

"There's a DVD in my apartment. Kelly next door has a key, you have my permission to enter and search my apartment for anything you like whenever you like. The DVD is, well shit, I'd better wait until you're there to tell you where it is. I really don't trust that this line is secure at your end. I can make more DVDs. I have the data here and in a couple places in the cloud, but I can't send it to you digitally until we can exchange encryption keys. He could find out too much about me from what I know about him. Once you have the DVD, I can give you the decryption key for it."

"Don't you think you're being a bit paranoid?" Morgan asked.

"I prefer it to being dead. How was Scott killed?"

"We can't give out that information," Morgan said.

"Was it quick? The last guy was burned alive," Sandra said.

There was a pause. "I don't think it was quick," Morgan said. "I'm sorry."

Sandra bit her lip. "Get over to my apartment. I'll know when you're there. I'll call you on my home phone. And tell Kelly to take the plecostomus. I won't be home for a while."

13

"Tell Kelly to take what?" Morgan asked.

"Tell him to take Rufus. He's got food for a couple weeks, but I'll probably be gone longer than that."

"I should remind you that you are a person of interest in a homicide, and fleeing the scene will not look good for you," Morgan replied.

"I was never at the scene," Sandra reminded him. "But I'm cooperating, and I will stay in touch. When do you think you can get down to my apartment?"

Jack had already brought the address up on the computer map. "Looks like 25 minutes."

"Great. Talk to you then," she said and clicked on the disconnect icon.

§

Sandra had 20 minutes to get on the road, get as far away from this location as possible, find another open WiFi access point, and get set up. She brought up the GPS map, and found the next small town, and started off.

I really need a shower, she thought as she pulled off the freeway. She was starting to get hungry but didn't want to walk into a restaurant the way she was. And fast food had no appeal. She watched the laptop as she drove around and found a signal from a coffee shop near a gas station. She pulled into the parking lot and moved to the passenger seat.

She set up the proxy, this time using a server in Chicago, since she needed more bandwidth and less latency in order to do video. The webcam server in her apartment came up on her browser, and she panned the camera around to scan the room. It had a wide-angle lens when zoomed completely out, but she zoomed in on key items to see if anything had been disturbed. Normally, any movement would have resulted in an email being sent to her with a short video, but she was not going to rely on that in the situation she was currently in.

The aquarium was still bubbling, and she could see the block of food for Rufus, but he was hiding. Her cell phone was where she had left it, the battery still sitting to the side. Cupboard doors were all still shut. Nothing was strewn around except those things she had decided not to pack at the last minute. It looked like no one had been there since she had left.

It was considerably longer than 25 minutes when the door opened. Kelly walked in, followed by a tall man with broad shoulders and a slim waist, whose head just cleared the doorway by an inch. A shorter man in much poorer physical condition followed behind him.

Sandra clicked on the call button. A moment later, the three men turned to look at the desk phone. The tall man picked it up.

"Jack Morgan, I presume," Sandra said, before he could begin a greeting.

"Ms. Millbarque. Cute trick," he answered.

"Call me Sandra, please, we're working together now. Or call me Sandy if you want to warn me that the bad guys are listening in. Nobody calls me that and lives. In the kitchen, in the top left cupboard is where I keep the cereal boxes. Get the Cap'n Crunch box and bring it back to the phone."

She watched as Jack handed the phone to the shorter man and walked into the kitchen. Kelly walked over to the aquarium and checked everything out, probably wondering how he was going to carry it into his apartment without spilling anything. After a while Jack came back with the cereal box and took the phone again.

"This one is unopened," he said.

"No, it's resealed," Sandra corrected. "I actually hate that kind of cereal, but it's a black hat inside joke. Do a search for John Draper sometime. If anything happened to me, my friends would know that Cap'n Crunch was out of place, and would get the joke, and look inside. Open it up."

Morgan handed the phone to the other man again and opened the box. He pulled out the bag of cereal and looked inside the empty box, and then felt the bag and found the DVD. He ripped open the bag and removed the disk. Kelly and the shorter man stooped down to pick up pieces of cereal off the floor.

Morgan found a pocket inside his jacket large enough for the DVD. He held the phone back up to his ear.

"I have the disk," he said.

"So I see," Sandra replied. "You and your friend can now have fun searching the place. You might want to help Kelly with the aquarium. It will be easier to move if you take most of the water out. I might have hidden the disk under Rufus's gravel, but everybody searches aquariums and wall sockets, it's in all the movies."

Morgan was searching the room for the camera, the phone still held to his ear.

"I'm over here," Sandra said, zooming the camera in and out so the servo gears would make noise. Morgan's eyes met the camera.

"Who's your friend?" Sandra asked.

Morgan touched the shorter man on the arm and pointed to the camera. "This is Jaime Gonzales, my partner," he said. Gonzales

16

squinted at the camera, and she panned it left and then right so he could see the movement.

"The camera is supposed to send me an email if it detects movement, and I haven't received any, so there's a good chance no one has been there since I left. On the other hand, if it was someone like me breaking in, the email would never get out of the room anyway, so we can't feel too sure of ourselves in that regard."

"Do you realize how paranoid that sounds?" Morgan asked.

"Occupational hazard in the computer security business. Nothing really works perfectly, or for very long. Always assume you or your equipment will screw up somewhere, and know your limitations. But also, it's a fun toy, and that's part of the attraction to the work. Playing with all the toys. That and outsmarting people smarter than me."

"Like killing your partner and blaming it on some imaginary serial killer?" Morgan asked.

"Wow, you *are* smarter than me," Sandra said. Then her tone changed. "Scott is a dear friend, and I would never want anything to happen to him. You have the disk. It has all my research on this guy and all of my methods, or at least the ones that are legal. Check it out. The guy is real, and he's after me now, and now that you have the disk, he'll probably be after you."

She took a breath, and changed her tone back to conversational. "Anyway, the disk has a bunch of tools on it as well as the data files. The one you need to run on your computer right away is called CleanSweep. It will scour your computer for things like keyloggers, and it will go out to the machines on your local subnet and scour them as well. It will keep guard on your network traffic to see if anything that goes out correlates with what you are typing, or what you typed since you last booted the machine. If he's managed to plant something on your computers, it has a good chance of finding it. And since I wrote it, he won't know about some of the things it can catch, so he might not be prepared for it."

"You seem pretty confident that he has already gotten into the computers at the station," Morgan said.

17

"It's the first thing I would have done," Sandra answered. "That is, if I was already planning something illegal in your neighborhood. Like killing someone."

Morgan looked up at the camera. Sandra suddenly felt very tired. And grubby.

"I'm going to sign off now," she said. "You guys have fun searching the place. Try not to break too much."

She clicked on the disconnect icon and watched as Morgan put the phone down. The first thing he did was walk over to the camera on top of the bookshelf and turn it towards the wall. She'd have to send Kelly a note to turn it back around when they had left.

She sent the decryption key to Jack Morgan's email address. Then she closed the laptop and moved into the driver's seat.

§

She had the GPS search for the nearest location of the gym she had a membership in. She was hungry but wanted to go someplace nicer than the places where she had recently dined. And a shower was currently more pressing than a meal.

Unfortunately, the nearest one was in Sacramento, an hour or two east of her current location. She got onto the freeway and headed east.

Three hours later, showered and refreshed, she sat alone at a table in a nice Italian restaurant, the laptop open, next to her plate of veal marsala. She was making a list.

Cash, transportation, housing, income. How had other people managed these things? She thought about all of the people she had tracked down, especially the ones who had lasted the longest out in the wild. *Learn from the best.*

By the time the table was cleared and the bill presented, she had some glimmerings of a plan. Tonight, it was sleeping in the car again. Tomorrow, a shower and new clothes, and then visit some banks.

She drove around until she found a quiet spot where she thought she wouldn't be disturbed until morning.

I need to call mom. Damn. It would be so much easier if mom had email at the new place.

She reached for her purse and remembered she didn't have her old phone, with her mother's new number in it. The events of the last few days caught up with her, and she buried her face in the sleeping bag, and let the tears come. *Why now? Why not in a couple months, after it was all over? Scott, I'm so sorry. Mom, Jen, I just can't do this.*

Chapter 4: I was a lot smarter before Anbar.

Gonzales took off his headphones. "No go. The call is coming from overseas, but the burner phone is in Redding, moving north at 75 miles an hour."

Jack frowned. "She wasn't in a car. I'd have heard a lot more noise."

He punched the number of the burner phone into the keypad, his other hand holding up the note it was written on.

"Busy," he said after a few seconds. "Ask them what number she's connected to right now."

Gonzales put the headphones back on and spoke into the microphone. He waited for several seconds.

"Thanks," he said to the microphone, and then to Jack he said, "The call to us wasn't from the burner phone. It was from somewhere in Malaysia. The burner phone is connected to (976) 468-6262."

"Where the hell is the 976 area code," Jack said, reaching for the computer keyboard. Then he stopped. "She's on a 976 line?"

Gonzales nodded.

"She probably gave the phone to some kid, and he's listening to dial-a-porn in his mom's back seat." Jack leaned back in his chair. "Have those guys figure out how she called from Malaysia," he said to Gonzales. "Then let's go surprise her next door neighbor."

A few minutes later, in the car on the way to Sandra's apartment, Gonzales asked, "Won't the guy be at work or something?" It was almost eleven o'clock.

"Maybe he's the manager," Jack said. "She seemed pretty certain he was going to be there."

"What if he's not there?"

"Then we'll need a warrant," Jack said. "But she's on record inviting us to search, we can play that to the judge."

"Actually, I don't think we can," Gonzales said. "I remember something about that."

"Then I guess he'd better be there," Jack said.

He was.

At their knock, Kelly Thompson opened his door and stared at the two men, not saying anything. He was wearing flannel pajamas and had bunny slippers on his feet. His hair looked like it hadn't been combed in a week. He looked up at Jack, and then down at Gonzales, and then up at Jack again, not saying a word.

Jack cleared his throat. "Sandra Millbarque said we could get the key to her apartment from you."

Thompson looked back over his shoulder into the room then back at Jack. A moment passed. "Oh, come on in," he said finally, in a voice that hadn't been in use for a while. He turned his back to them and walked into the room. Jack and Gonzales followed.

"I'd offer you some weed," he said, "but I ran completely out of it a couple days ago. I've been looking all over the place for even an old roach, you know, but the place is absolutely dry." He waved his hands around the room. It did indeed look like a thorough search had been done of the place. Perhaps by a band of chimpanzees. He turned around and began to sit, then fell down with a loud thump on a pile of laundry. Jack thought he looked stunned then realized that the expression on his face was the one he had met them with at the door. "I used to have a chair here," Thompson said.

"Have you seen anyone come or go out of Ms. Millbarque's apartment?" Jack asked the man on the floor.

"Yeah," Thompson answered.

"Can you be more specific?" Jack prodded.

"Sandra goes in and out," Thompson said.

"Anyone else?"

"Nah, she don't have anybody. I hit on her once, though. She said I was cute. Kissed me on the cheek. You know, like a grandma. Epic fail. I got Susie though. She puts out if I got weed." He nodded to himself and then started looking under clothing on the floor.

"The key?" Jack reminded him.

"It's still there," Thompson said.

"Where would that be?" Jack asked.

"What?"

"Where is the key?"

21

"In the fridge where it always is," Thompson answered. He went back to checking the pockets in the pile of laundry.

Jack picked his way into the kitchen. Surprisingly, the kitchen was clean. No dishes in the sink. No piles of anything on the floor. The stove looked unused, but recently cleaned. He ran a finger over the counter. No dust.

He didn't know what to expect when he opened the refrigerator. He held his breath and pulled open the door. The inside was spotless. Food was neatly wrapped and arranged in rows. Sandwiches and burritos, small bags of baby carrots and celery, juice boxes with straws glued to the sides.

In the door of the refrigerator were two glass jars where milk would normally be. One held a single key. The other held a folded paper with a pharmacy label on it. Jack looked closely at the label. It read "Medicinal Cannabis." There was nothing in the jar but the clean, neatly folded paper.

Jack took the other jar and closed the refrigerator door. He walked back out into the living room.

"Is this the key?" he asked.

"You gotta take it out of the jar first," Thompson said. "It's one of those old-fashioned keys."

"We're going to need you to open the door," Jack said. "It's a bit of a technicality."

"Oh, don't worry about that," Thompson said. "I used to be really good at mechanical stuff before I got blown up in Anbar. I still know how to work old-fashioned stuff."

He reached a hand up to Jack for assistance and, with the big man's help, managed to get up off of the floor. He took the jar, and turned it over a few times as if working out how it operated, and then opened the lid, and poured the key into his hand. Jack took the jar before it fell out of Thompson's hand, and then picked the lid up off the floor, and put them both on a shelf. Then he thought better of that and returned them to the refrigerator.

Thompson seemed pleased with the key and led the two other men out into the hallway to the door just down from his. He inserted the key, and opened the door in one slow, smooth movement, and stepped into the room. Jack followed, trailed by Gonzales.

Thompson had stopped three steps into the room, and the two men had to sidestep past him to close the door. The three men had been in the room for only a few seconds when the phone on the desk rang.

Jack held the phone to his ear and began to speak. But then he stopped.

"Ms. Millbarque," he said. "Cute trick."

Jack listened for a moment and then handed the phone to Gonzales.

He walked into the kitchen. Unlike the previous room, this kitchen had actually been used. Dishes had been set to dry in a rack next to the sink. A dishtowel was draped over the oven handle.

Jack started at the rightmost cupboard and opened each one in turn, examining the contents quickly but thoroughly, leaving the leftmost cupboard closed. He opened the refrigerator and noted that there was nothing in it that would spoil if left for a week. There was also no beer or wine, and none of the cupboards had held any alcohol either. He thought of where his wife had hidden her bottles when she started AA and made a mental note to search those places later.

When he had looked through everything else, he opened the leftmost cupboard. There was a row of cereal boxes, arranged by height. All the opened ones seemed to be from health food stores. The brightly colored one that stood taller than the others at the left of the row was an unopened box of Cap'n Crunch. He brought it back into the living room and took the phone from Gonzales.

"This one is unopened," he said. Then he handed the phone back and fought with the lid of the box, which did not seem willing to open easily. He ended up ripping it off, pulled out the bag of cereal, and looked into the empty box. He dropped the box onto the floor and felt the bag, probing with the fingers of both hands. He could feel the rectangular shape of a DVD box inside the bag. Expecting resistance, he pulled the bag apart forcefully. It shredded in his hands, cereal falling onto the floor. He found the

DVD and placed it in his inside coat pocket, the only pocket where it would fit. Gonzales handed him the phone and stooped down.

Thompson and Gonzales were picking up cereal off the floor, putting it back into the box along with the shredded bag. Jack spoke into the phone.

"I have the disk," he said. He listened and then began scanning the room. A buzzing of plastic gears on a bookshelf led his eyes to a small plastic Panda bear, its nose moving in and out as the gears drove it. Jack touched Gonzales on the arm and pointed to the toy on the shelf.

"This is Jaime Gonzales," he said. "My partner."

He listened to the phone. "Do you realize how paranoid that sounds?"

His eyes narrowed to a squint. "Like killing your partner and blaming it on some imaginary serial killer?"

He paused again to listen.

"You seem pretty confident that he has already gotten into the computers at the station," he said.

He listened again, and then looked up at the camera. The phone made a click, and he took it from his ear and returned it to the desk. Then he walked over to the Panda on the shelf, and turned it to face the wall.

§

Gonzales was already searching through the gravel at the bottom of the aquarium, his sleeves rolled up, but still getting soaked.

"That would be easier if you dumped out half the water," Jack said, starting in on the desk. He pulled out each drawer and checked under the desk in the space under the bottom drawers, one of his wife's favorite hiding places, large enough to hold a fifth of vodka lying down.

The contents of the drawers were surprisingly neat and spare, mostly extra power supplies, cables, and headphones for electronics. No paper. He looked around for a printer. There was no printer in the bedroom or the living room, and the small second bedroom, although crammed with electronics gear, also had no printer. *What has she got against paper?* Jack wondered.

He heard Gonzales lifting the top off the toilet tank. *I'll bet there's paper in there*, Jack thought, wearing his first grin of the day.

The small office made from the second bedroom was interesting. There were three huge computer monitors, connected to three different computers that were too big to fit on the table but stood on the floor next to it. Cables ran between the computers and all of their peripheral devices, the first sign of real untidiness Jack had seen in the apartment. There was a soldering station, a rack of expensive-looking test equipment, and several printed circuit boards strewn around the table, along with bits of wire and electronic parts. Stacks of plastic drawers were filled with more parts, each drawer with a little label made with the label gun sitting in the corner of the table. Jack opened each drawer but found nothing that didn't look like what the label claimed it contained, but Jack was not certain what those things were anyway.

The bedroom was unexciting. There was a bed, strewn with clothes she had decided not to pack. There was a headboard, where he found her cell phone and its battery. He put those in his jacket pocket. He removed the bedding and lifted the mattress, feeling around the underside for anything a mattress shouldn't have. He set the mattress up against the wall and lifted the box springs, listening for anything moving as he tipped it up. He checked all of the staples on the under-netting, and they all looked factory installed.

He checked the closet next. First all of the shelves, inside the shoes, pulling on shoe heels to make sure they would not open to reveal hidden spaces. He took down each garment on its hanger, checking the pockets for anything, then the seams. He found some old dinner mints, some loose change, a pen, and two business cards. He put the cards in his pocket and the loose change on one of the shelves.

He moved back into the bedroom and checked the dresser, removing the drawers and checking as he had with the desk in the living room. There were socks and underwear, folded pants, more shoes, and, in the bottom drawer, some condoms, lube, and a vibrator. *Forgot to pack these*, he thought, warranting a second grin.

In the bathroom, he checked all the drawers as methodically as the others. All the towels came out and were shaken, as were all the washcloths. He checked each bottle of cream and shampoo, holding them up close to the light to look for shadows of hidden objects if they weren't clear. The medicine cabinet had face creams, cleansers, and vitamins. No prescription bottles. Remembering the cereal box, he opened each box of toothpaste and tampons, checking inside. He checked inside the toilet paper roller. Gonzales had already checked the toilet tank, but Jack opened it again and shook the tank float to check for loose objects inside.

Jack looked at the scene of total disorder in the bedroom and bathroom and paused. Then he shook his head and started to put everything back the way it was.

Gonzales looked puzzled. "What are you doing?"

"If there *is* a killer looking for this lady, let's make him do the search all over again. She's got that camera in the living room, sounds alarms on her computer when someone comes in the door. She might be able to call us and get us over here before he's done. We can't rely on the vigilance of the neighbors, now, can we?" He looked past Gonzales at Thompson, who was staring at the wall.

26

Jack put the bed back together and neatly tucked in the sheets, blankets, and bedspread, followed by pillows and the decorative small pillows he had found on the floor. He hung up the clothes that had been tossed on the bed. Gonzales was neatly folding the towels in the bathroom.

Cleaning up took longer than the search itself, but when they were done, the apartment looked ready to show to a buyer or a date. Even the dishes in the sink were rewashed, dried, and put away, and the towel neatly hung on the oven door.

Jack took the notebook out of his pocket, looked something up, and then wrote down a phone number on a blank page and placed it near the desk phone.

"What's that?" Gonzales asked.

"The number to the burner phone we took from that bust a couple weeks ago. It's still in evidence. What do you want to bet it rings in the middle of the night sometime soon?"

"You gonna carry around a dead guy's phone all day, everywhere you go?"

Jack nodded. "If it doesn't help this case, it just might help that one."

Gonzales tapped the side of his head with his finger. "Smart."

Thompson looked away from the wall and spoke to Gonzales. "I used to be smart, too, before Anbar."

Jack walked over to the aquarium, still half empty. "Let's get this over to your place," he said. "You know you have to fill it with bottled water, right, not from the tap?"

Thompson nodded. "Chloramines," he said. "I'm good at taking care of fish. I'm the one who got Rufus for her, so she wouldn't be all alone all the time."

Jack held the aquarium in both hands and looked at the man. "Did she ever write anything down on paper?"

Thompson laughed. "Shit no," he said, as if that were obvious. "You can't encrypt paper."

They carried the aquarium back to Thompson's apartment, clearing a place for it on the dresser in his bedroom. Jack returned to lock the door of Sandra's apartment and then put the key back in the jar in the refrigerator.

27

"You call me if you think you hear someone going into her apartment," Jack said, handing his card to Thompson. "Don't try to stop him or let him know you're aware he's there, just call me."

Thompson took the card and was still staring at it as they closed the door behind them and walked down the hallway.

"Someone needs to get that boy some weed," Gonzales said.

Chapter 5: Six chambers, one bullet. Those are good odds, right?

"You want seven cashier's checks for five thousand each and the rest in cash," the bank teller said, showing no surprise or curiosity.

"Except a thousand has to stay in the account," Sandra said.

"I'm sorry, that's what I meant." The teller entered the transactions into the computer. "Made out to you, you said."

"That's right," Sandra replied.

It was a busy morning at the bank, with four tellers busy and a line of eight more customers waiting. Sandra looked up at the video cameras and wondered if Jack had run the CleanSweep program yet, and whether her bank transactions were being flagged and routed to him. He'd need a warrant for that, but more than enough time had passed for that. At least the funds had not been frozen. If they saw she was cleaning out her accounts, would she be stopped at the next bank, or the last one?

She could see most of the sidewalk outside through the big windows. There was a line at the autoteller. One of those people could be the client, waiting for her to leave. There hadn't been time for that.

She looked up at the cameras again. Airports had face recognition in real time. Banks didn't yet, as far as she knew. Aurora Flagg had defeated those by using Goth makeup to change her intraocular distance, and cotton pads in her cheeks to change the shape of her jaw. Something to remember if she was in an airport for some reason. Where else would they have face recognition?

"Would you like an envelope for these?" the teller asked, coming back with a sheaf of checks, tearing them at the perforations.

"Yes, please. And one for the cash."

The teller counted out the cash.

"And thirty eight cents," she said, handing Sandra the change. Why did I bother with change instead of leaving it in the account? Sandra wondered. Thinking about too many things at once. Slow down, or you'll mess up.

She had parked in the lot on the other side of the street, so she could watch her car while in the line. She tucked the envelopes in her purse, and walked out to her car, studying every face she found on her way out. No one jumped out at her or tried to steal her purse. She got into the car and locked the doors. She put the checks and cash into the glove compartment and locked it.

At the next bank, she left the uneven balance in the account and just took out checks. Always leaving enough in the account to forestall monthly fees, she went to the third bank and did the same. It was a blistering hot day in Sacramento, and she returned to the car drenched in sweat, even though the bank had been overly air-conditioned. She didn't relax until the car was moving, and she aimed the air vents at her arms and turned the air to MAX COLD.

The lawyer at the next stop was equally detached and outwardly uninterested in details.

"That kind of service will require a monthly retainer," the lawyer said, her voice professional and matter-of-fact. "We can put it on the books as an estate management fee, handled by a trust. You can call the trust anything you like, so your name is not involved directly in any correspondence. And you're protected by attorney-client privilege, of course."

"I'm not planning on breaking any laws," Sandra said. "And I haven't yet, as far as I know."

"Of course," the lawyer said. "But it is clear that confidential movement of funds is your principal concern, and we can structure things to maintain that confidentiality. As long as these amounts are not exceeded in any transaction or any monthly period."

"I understand," Sandra said.

She signed the power of attorney papers and handed over the cashier's checks. "I actually don't expect to need you to cash them, just mail them to me when you get my email."

"I understand. You *do* know you could have a friend or family member do this for you without the retainer fees, right?"

"It's obvious you haven't met my family," Sandra said. The lawyer smiled but looked concerned.

As Sandra left, the woman held her hand a little longer than normal for a handshake. "I hope things work out for you," she said.

"And if you need legal assistance for a divorce or a restraining order, our firm can help you out there as well."

Sandra squeezed the lawyers hand quickly and looked at the floor. "Thank you very much, I may be coming back for something like that."

The lawyer was blinking back tears. "Um, just, I mean, don't take matters into your own hands. Let the law help you."

Sandra hoped she hadn't overplayed her role. "Thank you," she said and left quickly.

On the way to lunch, she stopped at a Walgreens to get some more gift cards. While most of them clearly said Gift Card or some similar words, there were a few that looked more like real MasterCard and Visa cards. To get one that really looked like a credit card, she would need a physical mailing address. But she knew how to handle that, thanks to Jason Tyler. He had stayed on the run for 11 months.

In a dark quiet booth in a corner of a very well-appointed restaurant, she poked at her overpriced salad and connected to a proxy server in New Zealand on her laptop. Wellington was going to be her new mailing address, thanks to www.privatebox.co.nz.

For a small monthly fee, Private Box would provide a street address in Wellington, scan any mail that came in and email her the scans, or forward any mail in a new envelope or package to any address she chose. The scanning was optional, in case she didn't want their employees to actually open her mail. She was torn as to whether to use that particular service. Email was so convenient. But she left the box unchecked. What she needed from them at the moment was a physical credit card, and emailing that would not work anyway.

She paid for the service using the Visa number on the gift card. A $500 gift card would buy nine years of service. She hoped she wasn't going to need it that long. She paid for the first year up front, in case she had any trouble paying the bill monthly.

Using another $500 gift card, she signed up for a card online that would look more like a normal Visa card. It would be delivered to New Zealand. By the time it arrived, maybe she would have an address to send it to. She could always have it sent

31

to the lawyer's office, but she didn't plan to be anywhere near Sacramento for long.

With that in mind, she set up an account at Ridester. Walking through the process of setting up a one-way trip from Sacramento to San Jose, she chose the title "Deliver my car to San Jose," listed $0 as the cost, and left the date as flexible. She had to pull up another window to create a new email address in GMail to use for the notification, but other than that, it was easy to set up. Now she had to wait to see what kind of response she would get. *Too bad there isn't a way to tell them I would pay them to get it there*, she thought. Craigslist didn't seem to be the right place to do that, but she set up a job offer there anyway. A hundred dollars, plus transportation back.

Now to scour the web for ride offers to anywhere from Sacramento. Ridester did not have a way of entering only the departure zip code. She tried various cities at random as the destination and compiled a list of possible rides.

The first ride was with a man who had registered as DJ Cool. She passed on that one. The next one was soylent359. A movie buff? A science fiction fan? She responded to that one. She went down the list, not being especially choosy, responding to anything that looked vaguely safe, or had a female avatar. She left the Google Voice phone number on all of those she responded to, since it was now redirecting to the second pre-paid cell phone in her purse.

Now she had to wait for responses. A window popped up on the computer screen. "CleanSweep activated." The window listed an IP address and a MAC address, and a checksum. She wondered why Jack had taken so long to read the disk.

She left the restaurant and drove to a public library. Here it was cool, quiet, and had free WiFi. Se sat down at a table and started writing the eBook that Xavier was going to sell on the web to provide an income for her. *He's such a sugar daddy, that Xavier.*

Do-it-yourself Witness Protection, she wrote. *Poor William Thomas Johnson*, she thought. Would he have been safer if he had done his own witness protection? Could she write a book that would have saved him? The answer to that last part was a definite

32

yes. Combine Xavier's book with the federal protection program, and he would have stood a chance, at least until after the trial was over. *Don't use the damn loyalty cards.* Don't sell your privacy for a little discount on your groceries. Especially if your life is at stake.

She started listing the things someone would have to know about. All of the things that she had just been doing in the last two days. This was going to be easier than she thought. She'd been living this book since she found out about Bill Johnson's ill fortune.

She started sketching out notes for the book.

Don't break any laws. You might be hiding from an abusive spouse or a violently jealous husband, but you don't want to also be running from the police. They have more resources available to them than most people do.

Use indirection. Your mail is forwarded from an offshore address. Your phone is forwarded from an area code on the other side of the country. You place your funds in the hands of someone you trust, that the people who are after you don't know about.

Get an income. Sell stuff on eBay, or write a book. Have the checks go to your offshore address. Cash them in cities you are just passing through.

Get a pre-paid credit card that looks like a real Visa card. Some motels will let you pay with the card without presenting identification. Especially the ones that charge by the hour.

She was on a roll, typing fast, when the phone in her purse started buzzing. She grabbed up the computer and started walking to the restroom as she clumsily fished the phone out of her purse and whispered into it.

"Just a second, I'm in the library. I'll be able to talk in a second."

The voice on the other end whispered back "Oh. OK, I can wait."

She opened the door to the ladies' room. "You know, only one of us needed to whisper," she said in a more conversational tone. Her voice echoed off the tile.

"Oh. Sorry. Are you Sandra? How do you say your last name?"

"Mill bark," Sandra said. She realized she had screwed up and used her real name when soliciting the ride. That was stupid. Stupid was inevitable. Get over it. Just don't do it again.

"I'm Co --" she started and then reconsidered. "I'm leadvocals. We put an ad on Ridester called 'Ride with the Band.'"

"Yes, excellent. When are you leaving?" Sandra said.

"That's it?" came the voice on the other end of the phone. "Just like that? Great! We've been trying to get someone for four days, and they all back out when, I mean, great! We can leave as soon as you're ready."

"I just have to find someone who can drive my car back to San Jose for me. I offered a hundred bucks and airfare back, but no hits so far."

"You have a car?" the voice on the phone said. "Why do you need a ride?"

"Is that a problem?" Sandra asked.

"No! Not at all, just seemed funny, that's all. A hundred bucks to drive your car to San Jose? And a plane ticket back? I can find ten guys that would jump on that. Do they have to speak English?"

"I'm not particular," Sandra said.

"Give me, like, an hour, and I'll have someone for you, how's that? Should we come pick you up somewhere?"

"I can come to you," Sandra said.

"OK. We're at the Black Cat. That's a club downtown, you know it? It's in the Metro if you don't. Ask for, um, ask for Pocket. He's the drummer. If you get lost, here's my number," she said, and she read off the same digits that showed on the screen of Sandra's phone.

"I think I can find it," Sandra said. "I'll see you in an hour. Maybe less."

"Great! We have this gig in Vegas. We thought we might not make it in time. The bus uses so damn much diesel, we've been stuck here doing gigs for free so we can park in their lot."

"I'll see you then," Sandra said and disconnected.

What have I gotten myself into?

§

The GPS in Sandra's car knew about the Black Cat. It was only a twenty-minute drive from the library, and when she got there, she circled the block, taking in the neighborhood. She parked at a convenience store and walked down the sidewalk on the opposite side of the street, looking across at the venue. The front was painted black, but it had faded in the sun to a charcoal gray. The sign above the door probably looked better at night, lit from behind by fluorescent tubes. In the hot afternoon sun, it looked sad, despite the cheery efforts of the beer logo below it.

In the alley beside the club was a yellow school bus. Most of the windows had been painted black. A carefully hand-painted sign on the side of the bus read *Full Auto*. It looked more like an empty bus to Sandra.

That's my ride, Sandra thought. She could do worse. She remembered the words of the ride notice. *You pay gas.* No wonder they had found no takers. But they were travelling around the country, and only knew the first two cities they would hit. That was perfect for Sandra. Unpredictable, and not related to her in any way.

She crossed the street and knocked on the door. She waited a few minutes and knocked again. She was considering going around back to see if there was another entrance when the door opened just enough for most of a face to show.

"We don't open until eight," the face said.

"I'm supposed to ask for someone named Pocket," Sandra answered.

The face considered this then turned around. "Hey Pocket! Some chick at the door for you!"

The door did not open any farther. The face did not turn back around. Then it disappeared, and the door opened wider.

"You the chick wants to ride with the band?" a slender man in his early twenties, in jeans and a Metallica T-shirt, asked, while gesturing for her to enter. Sandra walked in past him, and the blast of hot air from the door ceased as it swung shut. The room was dimly lit, and she could see no details until her eyes adjusted. She stood there in the dark and felt Pocket walk by on her left.

35

"Coke is gonna be a while. She took the bike to get the guy that sweeps up. You wanna beer or something? The stuff on tap is free if they don't see you taking it."

"I think I'll be OK," Sandra said. The gloom was beginning to brighten, and she could make out tables and chairs, and a stage. Pocket was on the stage, walking towards the drum kit, behind the microphones and monitors.

She walked slowly towards the tables, taking care not to bump her shins on anything she could not see. The bass drum thumped loudly, and Pocket hit a tentative whack at the snare drum.

"You don't," he began, and then reconsidered, and started softly beating the snare in a complicated rhythm. He stopped after a few seconds and looked at her.

"I don't what?" she asked.

"Well, I guess most of our fans are, well..."

"Younger," she finished for him.

"Well yeah, but I didn't mean..."

"Don't worry about it," she said.

"I mean, you're pretty hot, I'm not saying, I mean, shit, I think I'll shut up now."

She smiled but couldn't tell if he could see that in the dim light.

"Tell me about your fans," she said.

"Well, they don't dress like that," he said. "I mean, all nice and shit, like some chick on TV. More tattoos, and nose rings, and blue streaks in their hair. And T-shirts that show their, well, T-shirts, and maybe black jeans. And make-up. Most of them look shitty without their makeup, I mean plain or something, not like you."

The bass drum thumped a few times, and he rattled a quick riff on the tom-tom.

"What kind of music do you play?" she asked.

"You never?" he started and then stopped. The bass drum woke up again, and he started to drum a complex set that kept coming back to the main beat, but with subtle changes between the returns. He kept it up for several minutes, and Sandra didn't think that any part of it actually repeated itself.

The face from the front door came out onto the stage, with a bass guitar slung low from the guitar strap, and plugged in and flipped the switch on an amplifier behind him. He nodded at Pocket and started to play. At first, he just accented the drumming, but then Pocket began to soften the beat and become more repetitive, and the bassist got more creative. The two played that way for another couple of minutes, and then the lights came on, and the music stopped clumsily, like a stack of beer cans falling over.

Sandra turned around and saw a striking young woman walking towards the stage, with shining long black hair with a shock of dark crimson on the side. She was wearing tight black jeans and a short-cut T-shirt, and she was followed by a small man in a denim jacket and dirty jeans.

The woman stopped at Sandra's table. "You must be her," she said, holding out her hand.

"I must be," Sandra said, taking the hand and standing up.

"This is Rafael," the woman said. "He's interested in the job. Driving to San Jose."

"Great," Sandra said, extending a hand to Rafael. He shook her hand quickly but gently, his calloused hand rough in hers.

"He says if you can give him the money for the plane, he'd rather have that, and take the bus back."

Sandra nodded to the man. "How about two hundred then, for the whole trip? You drop the car off at my apartment, in parking space 32? I have a friend there who can drive you to the bus."

He nodded his head vigorously, but the woman translated anyway. "I'll write that down for him," she said, reaching for a napkin from the bar.

Sandra took her wallet out of her purse, and counted out ten twenty-dollar bills, and set her keys on top of them.

"That's pretty gutsy," the woman said, handing the napkin to Rafael. "You just met the guy."

"You trust him, right?" Sandra asked.

"You just met me," the woman said.

"Actually, I haven't," Sandra said. "I don't even know your name."

"Cocayne Phillips," the woman said, holding out her hand again. "With a 'Y', not like the nose dust. People call me Coke, or they don't call me."

"Your mother gave you that name?" Sandra asked.

"Nope. But she never was all that creative. Or bright. Where's your car?"

"In the GasNGo lot across the street. Silver Lexus."

The woman looked at Sandra for a moment. "You better give Rafael your cell phone number, in case he gets stopped, and they think he stole it."

"It's (505) DEDUCES," Sandra said, pulling out her phone. "I always have to look at the keypad to figure out what that is in digits."

"333-8237," the woman said. "It's a prime number. The last four digits, that is. I can't do seven digits. I called you already, remember?" She wrote the number down on the napkin and handed it back to Rafael.

"You factored that in your head?" Sandra asked.

"I wish. My phone can do it, but only to 10,000. I like to play with numbers. Your stuff in the bus or still in the car?"

"Still in the car."

"Rafael will get it," she said, waving the man away. He nodded and hurried towards the door.

"Is Link back yet?" she asked Pocket.

"Not yet," came the answer.

"Soon as he's back, we can blow," she said. She looked at Sandra. "If that's good for you."

Sandra shrugged. "I'm good, whatever you like."

"You hungry? I'm gonna nuke some wings. There's chips and shit. Not much else."

Pocket jumped down from the stage. "I'm in," he said.

The bass player unplugged, and turned off the amplifier, then joined them at the bar.

"Charlie Dobbs," he said, offering his hand to Sandra.

"Sandra Millbarque," she said. "But I'm thinking of changing that."

"Cool," said Pocket.

Cocayne met her eyes. "You don't play it real safe, do you?"

Sandra held her gaze and considered. "Six chambers, one bullet. Those are good odds, right?"

§

The drums and amplifiers had been loaded into the bus and secured, and all the windows pulled open to cool off the roasting interior when a tall, thin man with long, brown hair and a trimmed beard arrived with a two-gallon can of diesel fuel. His shirt was wet with sweat in streaks. He looked at the group standing in the shade of the bus but said nothing as he opened the fuel cap and lifted the can to fill the tank.

Cocayne Phillips touched Sandra on the arm and walked towards the young man.

"Link, this is Sandra, at least for now. Sandra, this is Lincoln Spencer."

The young man nodded at Sandra. "You got gas money?" he asked, setting down the empty fuel can.

"Yeah, just a second," she said, getting her wallet out of her purse.

"Say hello to the nice lady, Link," Cocayne said, pushing on his shoulder.

"It's hot," he said. "God I'll be glad to be out of this place. Hello, Sandra."

"Hello, Link," Sandra said. "It is friggin' hot. Take this." She handed him one of the gift cards. "It's good for about four hundred. Let me know if it stops working, and I'll fill it up again."

Lincoln Spencer took the card and looked at it, then turned it over. "Cool," he said. He looked at Sandra again and seemed much less annoyed.

"Let's get the bike stowed, and we can get out of here," Cocayne said.

The three men wrestled with lifting the small motorcycle up onto the rack on the back of the bus and cinching the tie downs tight. Cocayne pulled the thick cable of a lock through the wheel spokes and clicked it shut.

The inside of the bus had been modified considerably since its days of hauling kids off to school. The seats had been removed, and in their place were two couches, six pull-down cots bolted to the walls, a small refrigerator, a sink, and a bathroom that looked like it had been removed from a recreational vehicle with a chainsaw. There was a large net hung from the ceiling in the rear quarter of the bus, and sleeping bags and duffle bags were thrown up into it at random. The pull-down cots had been lowered to allow air to flow through the windows, and only the center aisle of the bus was actually clear enough to stand up in. Sandra walked to the back of the bus, where a kitchen table was bolted to the floor, and slid into the bench seat, and put her purse and computer on the table. Cocayne sat up front on a couch, leaning on an elbow because the cot would not let her sit up straight. Link was in the driver's seat. Charlie and Pocket had each climbed onto a cot opposite one another, close to Sandra, and were quietly staring at her. She pretended not to notice.

Link drove the bus a few blocks to the station where he had filled the jerry can and got out to fill the tank using his new card. Cocayne walked down the center of the bus and poked Pocket in the ribs. "Knock it out, you two." she said and slid into the bench seat opposite Sandra.

"I'm not going to ask a lot of questions," Cocayne said. "You share what you like, that's OK. But I'm pretty observant, and I jump to conclusions really well. If you're in trouble, maybe we can help."

Sandra was ready with her cover story. "My ex is a cop. I'm trying to avoid him at the moment."

"So you're ditching your car and not using your credit cards," Cocayne said. "Is Rafael going to get in trouble when he drops off the car?"

"No, my friend Kelly lives there," Sandra said. "Jack won't be expecting the car to show up in Kelly's parking spot."

"Jack is the ex?"

"Jack Morgan," Sandra explained. "He's a homicide detective."

"He beat you up or something?"

"No, it's not like that. It's complicated," Sandra said.

"I've done complicated," Cocayne replied, leaning sideways on the bench, resting her elbow on the table, her head on her hand.

"So," Pocket said from the cot behind Cocayne, "you're single then."

"And off limits," Cocayne said. "God, you two are such horndogs. Give it a rest."

Link got back in the bus and started it up.

"So, you're playing in Las Vegas?" Sandra asked.

"A little dive in Henderson, actually," Cocayne said. She waved her hand, encompassing the interior of the bus with her gesture. "We're not exactly some hot attraction."

"Speak for yourself," Charlie said. Cocayne ignored him.

"We make some money selling CDs on our Facebook page, and we get enough gigs to keep us fed. Sometimes enough to actually gas up. Beats a day job though."

The bus picked up speed, and the wind started blowing through the windows, sweeping Cocayne's long hair into her face.

"Let's get those bunks tied up, and get the windows shut," she said, sliding off the bench seat into the center aisle. The two musicians slipped off the cots and raised them up against the windows, then pulled the windows shut. Cocayne walked forward and tied the other two cots up against the wall, and Charlie and Pocket walked the length of the bus, shutting the windows.

"Link, crank that AC up," Cocayne called up front, while rejoining Sandra at the table. "You two might want to get some sleep," she said to the two young men. "It's at least ten hours to Henderson, and I'm taking second shift, so one of you is going to be doing the dawn shift."

"I'll take it," Charlie called out, stretching out on the couch up front. "Pocket can owe me."

Chapter 6: If the guy had just stayed dead, they wouldn't have shot him.

The DVD sat on the kitchen table as Jack looked up *keylogger* on Wikipedia. He read the article slowly and carefully, occasionally looking up technical terms he was unfamiliar with.

So keyloggers are a bad thing. If Millbarque's client had infected computers at the station, there was a good chance his laptop was also infected, since he used it at work frequently. He turned off the WiFi switch on the computer and reached for the DVD. If his computer was infected, at least it wouldn't be reporting home.

He inserted the DVD into the player. The disk spun up, and a window popped up on the screen, but the screen went black before he could read it. The laptop was rebooting.

Great, he thought.

He waited for the machine to recover and logged back in. A window popped up listing the contents of the DVD. The first directory was named CleanSweep. Below that was a directory titled BlackHat. Jack typed in the decryption key and opened that directory. The list of files there was huge. He opened each of the first four files, but they contained logs of numbers and dates that meant nothing to him. He looked down the list and found a file labeled *notes.html*. This one he could read.

Phone numbers he has received calls from.

Phone numbers he has called.

IP addresses receiving encrypted text.

IP addresses sending encrypted text.

Johnson.

Haggerty.

Malone.

Simonson.

Connections between victims.

Possible clients.

Always a different M.O.

Always flies first class.

Likes to rent muscle cars.

List of stolen identities.

List of stolen credit cards.

43

Access points used near victims.

No bank account, no bank visits.

Statistically unlikely purchases:

Bruichladdich Black Art Cask Strength Single Malt.

Lined Lamb Textured Palm Driving Glove.

Cartier Santos-Dumont Watch.

Federal Premium Hydra-Shok 9 mm Luger 147 Gr. HSJHP 1000 rounds

The list went on for several pages. Most of the entries were links to other files on the disk, including the lists of numbers and dates.

All circumstantial. Nothing concrete. But at first glance, it did seem to be very difficult to come to any other conclusion. These people were killed by a hit man, and all by the same one, and he was likely hired by clients with different associations, so he wasn't a mob guy. And he had killed two federal agents who had been protecting a witness, and had killed a second witness under protection. If nothing else, Millbarque knew far too much about the witness protection program than was good for anybody. She had found someone under federal protection, and he was dead.

This was no longer a local matter. Much as Wilson would hate it, this had to go to the marshals.

He called Chief Wilson at home.

"It looks like the Tremain thing is connected to two federal marshal cases, including agents killed," he said, after perfunctory greetings.

"The gumshoe guy with the no footprints?"

"That's him. He was tracing someone who happened to be in WITSEC, and managed to find him. Then he reports the location to his client, and the WITSEC guy ends up dead. Then he starts investigating the client, and gumshoe ends up dead."

"Is this stuff solid?"

"Circumstantial so far. Computer files. Gumshoe didn't know the guy was in WITSEC."

"How the hell did he find him, then?"

"I'm working on that," Jack said.

"Better send what you have to the marshals, set up a meeting. They'll want to take lead on it, if they buy your angle."

"I know. I've worked for worse," Jack said.

"Bet your ass you have," Wilson replied.

Jack disconnected and called Gonzales.

"You looked at it, didn't you," Gonzales said, not bothering with a greeting.

"I did," Jack admitted.

"We said we were going to give it to the lab guys first, let them check it out."

"I turned off the Internet gadget first. If anything is compromised, it's only my computer," Jack said.

"Listen to you, like you know anything about that shit. You saw the chick's setup. She's a pro. You got hacked already."

"I didn't run the program she told me to run. All I did is look at some files," Jack countered.

"You're buying her whole story, I can tell."

"No way. She's in this up to her eyeballs. There's a ton of stuff on the disk, she's been tracking this guy for months. Then all of a sudden, she panics and bolts, and her boss ends up dead at the exact same time. I don't think he knew she was tracking their meal ticket. He might still be alive if she hadn't been snooping. But there's nothing on the disk that says anything about why she bolted."

"So she's not coming clean with us," Gonzales stated.

"Not by a long shot."

"You think maybe she's working with the hitter?"

"I can't rule it out," Jack said. "But we'll be free of all this anyway. The marshals are going to want to work it."

"You talked to the chief?"

"Yeah. He took it pretty well, but he'll be pissed in the morning," Jack said.

"He's always pissed in the morning," Gonzales said.

"That too. See you in the morning then."

"Oh boy," Gonzales said, and disconnected.

§

Gonzales and Chief Wilson were talking to two men in the small conference room when Jack arrived with his computer under his arm. Wilson scowled at being kept waiting but didn't let the marshals know he was upset with Jack.

The fat marshal spoke first, before being introduced. "Is that the PI's computer?" he asked, reaching for the laptop in Jack's hands.

"No," Jack said, pulling the computer away and then setting it down on the table. "This is my computer. I brought it in so we can look at the files."

"We're going to need the PI's computer," the fat man said.

"No problem," Jack said. "You have complete access to everything we have."

"Good luck with that," Gonzales said. "The guys in the lab say it's all encrypted."

Wilson scowled at Gonzales, who stepped back.

"You'll probably want this, too," Jack said, handing the DVD to the fat man.

"What's this?"

"Those are the files we could read. That's the original disk, entered into evidence just a few minutes ago."

Jack looked at Wilson. That's why I was late, boss. Chain of custody.

"This tells how they got into WITSEC?" the other marshal asked.

"I haven't had any of the computer guys look at it," Jack said, hoping they wouldn't see the evasion.

"Any copies of this lying around? We'll need those." Fat man seemed a little more belligerent than necessary.

"No one in the precinct has made any copies," Jack said. "But there may be copies out in the wild somewhere. Or on the computer in evidence, that we can't seem to read."

"Get that computer," the fat man said to the other marshal. The man nodded but stayed where he was.

"You understand," the fat man said to Wilson, "that any breach in federal security has to be kept under tight wraps until we can

46

patch the holes. Two witnesses under federal protection are dead, along with two federal marshals."

Wilson looked the fat main in the eye and set his stance just a bit wider. "I imagine that looks pretty bad on your resume," he said. Jack winced inside but was careful not to let anything show.

The fat man tried to stand taller, and his voice got a little louder than the small room warranted. "We're going to need everything you have on this. Reports, evidence, witnesses, that computer, this thing," he said, waving the disk, "and anything else that might possibly be relevant." He looked at the three locals in turn. "And no copies left behind."

"We'll need that last part from a judge," Wilson said. "We aren't in the habit of destroying evidence around here."

"This meeting is over," the fat man declared, and he and the other marshal walked out of the room and could be heard barking for the desk sergeant a few seconds later.

"That seemed to go well," Gonzales said.

§

Jack brought his computer to the coffee house as he and Gonzales left the marshals probing through the evidence locker. The morning had been every bit as unpleasant as Jack had expected, and as Wilson and the marshals could make it. He opened up the notes.html file and pushed the computer over so that Gonzales could see.

"I thought you said you didn't make any copies," Gonzales said.

"I said no one at the precinct had made any copies," Jack explained. "I made this copy when I was at home."

Gonzales made a face. "I hope your lawyer is better at splitting hairs than you are."

"Check this out," Jack said, and brought up a page.

Gonzales studied it for a while. "So?"

"How did she get all the phone numbers he's called? From six burner phones?"

"And all the calls to those phones," Gonzales said.

"The marshals are going to have all they need to hold her, just on that," Jack said.

"Once they find her."

"Yeah. Good luck with that," Jack said, echoing Gonzales' earlier comment.

He brought up another page. "Here's her list of guesses at who hired him."

"Which one's the guy a witness against?" Gonzales asked.

"None of them. The guy was going to testify against Carlo Melone. He's a Mexican drug cartel guy, in prison already for a drive-by a couple years ago. Four life sentences. Unlikely he has money for a hit man, and what more are they going to do to the guy anyway?"

"So Melone knows something and wants a favor from his old bosses," Gonzales said.

"Why was the guy in WITSEC in the first place?"

"You'll never get that out of the marshals," Gonzales said.

"Not a chance. But I know someone who's still working the case," Jack said.

Gonzales looked at the smile on Jack's face. "You mean the chick."

"Sandra Theresa Millbarque. She's way ahead of all of us on this."

"Until she gets herself killed," Gonzales said.

"My money's on the lady who can track a hit man's cell phone without a warrant," Jack said.

Jack flipped the switch to enable the WiFi on his laptop and connected to the coffee shop's access point. "Let's find out what the newspapers have on William Thomas Johnson," he said.

A window popped up on the screen. "CleanSweep: Connection not secure. Enable proxy?"

"What's that about?" Gonzales asked.

"I didn't copy that directory," Jack said. "I just copied the BlackHat directory."

"And that name didn't ring any alarms in your brain?" Gonzales asked.

"That's her name for the bad guy," Jack said. The popup window timed out.

"CleanSweep: Proxy enabled. Connection is secure."

"So how did this thing get on your computer?" Gonzales asked.

"The computer rebooted right after I put the disk in," Jack said.

Gonzales slapped the table. "There you go. This chick is bad news."

Jack flipped the switch back off. "Let's not use this computer to get online," he said.

Gonzales pushed his seat back to his plate and picked up his sandwich. "What did she say the program was going to do?"

"Check for keyloggers. Things that record everything you type and send it to the bad guys." Jack moved the cursor and checked the list of installed programs.

"Well, she wasn't hiding it," he said, and clicked on the *Report* menu item under the CleanSweep entry.

"28 problems found. 28 problems fixed. See log for details."

Jack read the log. "It says zero keyloggers found," he said. "But there's all this other shit about security holes patched and vulnerabilities eliminated."

"Maybe it's a good thing you ran the program," Gonzales offered.

"It hasn't started erasing all my files," Jack said, flipping the switch back on and reconnecting to the Internet. The CleanSweep window popped up again. He clicked on OK.

William Thomas Johnson had reportedly been killed in a drug-related shooting in Los Angeles. Jack could not find an obituary notice, just the crime report. There were obituaries for the other two victims.

"So, was he dead the first time or the second time?" Gonzales asked.

"Not the first time. That's when he went into WITSEC. They wanted everyone to think he was dead. Apparently he wasn't dead enough to hide from Millbarque."

"So if he had just stayed dead, they wouldn't have shot him the second time," Gonzales said.

"Maybe the first time wasn't related to Melone at all. If you were the marshals, and you thought someone on the inside was leaking WITSEC information, wouldn't you want to mess with the records a little bit and not link the guy to the real target?"

"So the chick is paying someone in the marshals to leak WITSEC locations?" Gonzales asked.

"I don't think so. How would she figure out that the witness against Melone was her guy? No, I think she has some other way of finding the WITSEC people. Just like she said on the phone. Something about stuff they bought."

"Like 'statistically unlikely purchases,'" Gonzales offered.

"Yeah, like that." Jack brought up the notes.html file again. "Like someone who flies first class, likes Scotch, Cartier watches, and a thousand rounds of big-ass 9-millimeter bullets."

"She was using the same trick on the hitter," Gonzales said.

"So it would seem," Jack concurred.

A window popped up on the screen. "CleanSweep: 3 compromised computers found on local subnet." The window offered choices of *Repair, Isolate, Eliminate,* and *Ignore.* The second choice was highlighted. Jack was contemplating what to do when the window timed out and went away.

50

"She doesn't give a guy a lot of time to think," he said to Gonzales.

"CleanSweep: 3 compromised computers isolated."

Jack turned off the WiFi switch and closed the laptop. Two tables down, a man looked over at Jack and asked, "Your Internet go down too?"

Jack nodded, and he and Gonzales got up to leave.

§

When Jack and Gonzales arrived back at the station, Jimmy Wallace met them at the door. The younger detective stopped the two men with his arm.

"I'm not sure you two want to go in there right now," he said. "The marshal is screaming at the chief, and your name keeps coming up," he said, pointing to Jack. "Something about a disk that crashed all the computers."

Jack looked at Gonzales. "You stay here if you want. I'm going to go in and straighten things out."

"Are you kidding? I wouldn't miss this for Super Bowl tickets."

As they walked through the station, Jack was aware of every eye in the place either staring at the pair or suddenly looking elsewhere. The computers he could see looked fine, and people seemed to be working at them normally. They made their way to where the shouting was going on. As they turned a corner, the fat marshal saw Jack and shouted.

"You! Of all the stupid, negligent, incompetent things! You brought this thing in here!" he said, waving the disk in the air.

The more upset the man seemed to get, the calmer chief Wilson seemed to get. Jack made a note to remember that. If you wanted Wilson to be cool and rational, make sure there is some idiot in the room getting hysterical.

"Apparently there's something on the disk that crashed all the computers in the station," the chief explained.

"On that disk," Jack asked, pointing to the DVD the marshal still held up in the air. "The disk of evidence removed from a skip tracer that uses the Internet to find people in witness protection?"

The fat marshal brought his hand down and looked at the DVD.

"Let me get this straight," Jack continued. "You waited until I was safely out of the building, and then you took a computer disk that came from an Internet hacker, and you put it into a police computer, one that was still connected on the network to all of the other computers in the building, and you didn't think that there was anything wrong with this idea? And you're saying that I'm the one that is stupid, negligent, and incompetent?"

The fat man reddened. "I don't like what you're insinuating," he started.

"If you like, I'll stop insinuating and spell it out for you," Jack said. "But as luck would have it, our computers are all protected by our new CleanSweep program, and we can assess the damage and see if we have anything to charge you with."

Jack turned to the screen on the desk and moved the mouse to bring up the CleanSweep report menu.

"418 problems found. 418 problems fixed. See log for details."

Jack clicked on the button to bring up the log.

"6 keyloggers found: implementing countermeasures. 17 Trojans found and removed. 395 security vulnerabilities found and repaired." The log went on to list them in detail for several pages.

"You seem to have lucked out," Jack said, turning to the marshal. "Our software found and fixed all the problems you caused."

He turned to the chief. "If I could suggest that this man not be allowed to use department computers for the duration of his stay, I think it might keep things running a little smoother around here." He winked at the chief in a way that the marshal could not see and walked back to his desk. Gonzales followed.

"Our new CleanSweep program?" Gonzales asked, in a low voice.

"Did you see the log?" Jack asked. "She was right. Six keyloggers. Some asshole has every password in the station and has been watching everything typed on every computer in the place." He reached for the phone and punched four quick digits.

"Jimmy, what's the number of the IT guy? We need to get him to make sure everyone changes their passwords right away.

Probably all their passwords for things outside the station too, like bank accounts, email, all that stuff. Blame it on the marshal that crashed all the computers this morning. Hell, you just call him, I'm going to be busy. And tell him the marshals installed a new program called CleanSweep to clear up the mess and prevent anything like that from happening again."

"I'm not sure I want to be around you when this comes back to bite your ass," Gonzales said.

"What?" said Jack, feigning ignorance. "Who installed the CleanSweep program while we were at lunch? The marshal did. Who crashed all the computers while we were out of the building? The marshal did. Who found out we had four hundred-odd viruses on our computers? Little old Jack did. I think we come out smelling like roses."

"You just got really, really lucky," Gonzales said.

"I don't think luck had anything to do with it," Jack said. "I'm just that brilliant. I just wished I'd planned the whole thing."

"We know who really did that," Gonzales said.

Chapter 7: There was a tear of some regret, when the bullet met her man.

Sandra was drifting in and out of sleep as the bus gently rocked with each passing big rig. The noise of the tires and the passing cars sounded like surf on the beach, and she was dreaming of Tahiti when the buzzing brought her awake. The phone in her purse was set to vibrate. She dug the phone out, wondering what her sister was doing calling at three o'clock in the morning.

It wasn't her sister. It was her own voice that she heard on the phone.

"Power is out," she heard herself say. "Motion detected."

The servers in her apartment were running on backup power. And someone was moving around in her office. At three in the morning. She sat up and bumped her head on the ceiling of the bus loudly. She climbed down from the high bunk and carried the phone back to the table where she had left her computer. "Shit," she said quietly to herself, realizing there would be no Internet connection. She called information on the phone. *Call Jack. If you call Kelly, the client might hear the phone ringing at three in the morning next door and put two and two together.*

There was a Jack Morgan on Morley Street. She called the number. After four rings, a machine answered, and Jack Morgan's voice said simple "Speak."

"Jack, pick up the phone. Someone's in my apartment and they've cut the power. Get your butt over there and you can nail this guy. Pick up the phone."

She waited for the beep, and then hung up and pushed redial.

"Wake up, Jack. The perp is in my house. He's cut the power. He's in my server room. Get your butt out of —"

"I'm up," Jack said, cutting her off.

"You have to get over to my apartment," Sandra said, trying to keep her voice low.

"I'm going to hang up," Jack said. "And call for a patrol car. They can get there a lot faster than I can."

"Of course," Sandra said. "I'm hanging up." She pushed the button on the phone to end the call.

She pictured what was going on in her apartment. He'd cut the power, and probably the phones, but he hadn't thought to bring a

54

cell phone jammer. The cell phone hidden in her server had still managed to place the call to (505) DEDUCES.

So calling Kelly probably wouldn't have worked anyway. He only had the landline.

What would happen next? Jack would tell the patrol officers that the perp was armed and dangerous. Would they come in with sirens blaring and give him enough warning to get away? Would they wait for backup and give him time to slip out? He was not going to be long in the apartment. She knew what he'd be after.

"Hey," Pocket said sleepily, walking up behind her. "Everything OK?" Pocket was dressed only in Spiderman boxer shorts but did not seem to notice or care.

"Yeah," she said, still keeping her voice low.

"Who's Jack? That your ex, the cop?"

"Shhh," she whispered, pointing to Charlie's bunk, and the couch where Link was stretched out.

"You messing with him? Pranking him in the middle of the night?"

"Something like that," she said.

"Cool," Pocket replied. He yawned.

"Go back to bed, Pocket," Sandra said quietly.

"OK," he said and padded off, his bare feet making little sound on the rubber floor of the center aisle.

Sandra pulled the computer over and swiped her finger on the mouse pad to wake it up. She entered Jack's home phone number in a file, reading it off the cell phone display. Then she removed the battery from the phone. *Have to get another couple phones in the morning. And a 5G Internet connection. Have to get someone in the band to sign for that.*

She looked around for a way to charge her computer, but there were no AC outlets in the bus. *Pick up a marine battery and inverter too.*

She walked back to the high bunk and climbed up, putting the phone and battery back in her purse.

I hope they shoot the guy. Poor Scott. She still did not know how Scott Tremain had died.

Somehow, she drifted off to sleep.

Chapter 7: There was a tear of some regret, when the bullet met her man.

§

The bus slowed as it left the off-ramp, and Sandra awoke just before the bus turned so that the morning sun hit her square in the face. She held her hand up against the glare and looked around.

Charlie Dobbs was driving, and Cocayne had stretched out in the bunk opposite hers. Link had also awakened, and Pocket was already up and dressed. Sandra swung her feet over the edge of the cot and banged her head on the ceiling again.

Her clothes were a wrinkled mess from sleeping in them. *I've got to get something more practical for this lifestyle.* She looked over at Cocayne, who seemed to be wearing nothing but a long T-shirt. *Maybe not that practical.* She looked back at Pocket, who was brushing his teeth in the little sink. She did the same when he was done.

The bus was negotiating early morning traffic, and she walked forward to stand next to Charlie as he drove. "So," she said, keeping her voice low, "What is the plan for the day?"

"Probably set up and practice," Charlie said. "What we usually do when we hit a new gig. If you screw up the first night, they don't come back."

"I'm trying to plan my own day," she said. "I'm going to need to get on the net, get some clothes, get a few other items. I suppose I'll be getting a cab. Is there anything you'd like me to pick up for you while I'm out?"

"There's usually plenty of beer at the gig," Charlie said. "So I think we're probably OK. You could ask Cocayne, she's the one who usually thinks of all that stuff."

"Ask me what," Cocayne's voice came from close behind Sandra. Sandra turned to see Cocayne in her T-shirt and bare feet, standing behind her.

"If there's anything I can pick up for you while I'm out shopping," Sandra said.

"Coffee," Cocayne said, yawning and stretching.

"You got it," Sandra said. "And if you get time for a break, I'd like to buy you a 5G router, so we can have Internet on the road."

"You mean buy you one of those," Cocayne said. "I don't know what that is. My phone has Internet."

"It's like a phone. It gets Internet over the air like a cell phone does, but then it acts like a WiFi hotspot and gives Internet to other computers on the bus, like my laptop."

"So you did mean buy you one of those," Cocayne said.

"Actually, I was hoping to put it under your name. I pay for it, but my name doesn't show up where a particular person could find it."

"Ah, things begin to become clear," Cocayne said. "Talk to me around lunchtime. You buy us all a nice lunch somewhere that isn't a beer joint, and you could probably talk me into anything."

"Sounds good to me."

Charlie raised his voice. "Help me out, people. Somewhere on this road is a dive called the Broken Pony. Shout if you see it."

They all looked around at the street. It was not particularly inviting, partially industrial, some faded retail.

Link came up behind Cocayne. "Must be getting close, there's a Bail Bond place."

"Oh shut up," Cocayne said, elbowing him. "You get us the next gig, if you're so special."

"Found it," Charlie said, slowing the bus and pulling into the turn lane to make a left.

The Broken Pony looked as faded as the rest of the buildings on the street. There was a huge empty parking lot between it and a medical clinic. There was a barber shop on the other side. Charlie pulled the bus up next to the back door. Everyone piled out of the bus into the early morning heat. *This is going to be every bit as hot as Sacramento.*

Cocayne and Link were at the back door when it opened, and a young woman came out, carrying a mop and a bucket on wheels. "You guys the band?" she said. "Lou said you'd be here around lunch time."

"We're *Full Auto*," Cocayne said. "You got a place for us to set up?"

As the men carried in amplifiers, drums, and instruments, Sandra found a table and opened her laptop. There was no WiFi signal. So much for getting the news of last night. She was not about to use the cell phone in a place where they might be staying

58

for several days, or maybe even more. She used the phone at the bar to call a cab.

"I'll be out running errands," she told the group. "Getting coffee," she said to Cocayne. "I'll be back to take you out to lunch. Someplace nice. My treat."

They all gave perfunctory goodbyes, busy carrying microphone stands and setting up. She went outside to wait for the cab.

When it came, she got in and said, "Can I have you for the whole morning? I have a bunch of things to do. Starting with a shower."

The driver did not think there was a branch of her gym in the area. And he didn't like the idea of the by-the-hour motel. "A lady like you shouldn't go into one of those places. I could take you there, but I couldn't just leave you at the door. Who knows what would happen."

In the end, she agreed that he could come with her and wait outside the door to the room while she used the shower. The room was actually much nicer than she had imagined, not any different from a Motel 6 or a Best Western. The shower was clean. There was shampoo and a hair dryer, and freshly laundered towels that looked new. She came out of the room feeling much better, wearing a wrinkled but otherwise fresh blouse and pants. A quick stop for a breakfast burrito, and she was almost her old self again.

The next stop was a shopping center, where she bought clothing that was mostly knits and jeans, that would stay looking reasonable if slept in, and some modest sleeping apparel that didn't look like pajamas. She had noticed the bus had no coffee maker, so she bought one. She bought three more cheap, pre-paid cell phones and threw away the one she had used the night before. But she kept its battery.

After that was an auto parts store, where she bought a marine battery and a 1,000-watt inverter. More than enough for the laptop and the coffee maker, but she planned to get a small microwave and a toaster as well. That was the next stop. The cab driver helped her with the big battery and put it into the trunk.

"Last two things," she said as they headed back to the Broken Pony. "Where's a really nice place for lunch nearby, and where is the nearest place to that I can get a Verizon phone?"

At the Broken Pony, the driver helped her get the battery, inverter, coffee pot, microwave, toaster, and groceries into the bus. She paid him, tipping generously, and set about installing the inverter as he drove away. The bus had 12-volt wiring for lights and cigarette lighter outlets near the sink. She connected a charging cord to the battery and plugged it into one cigarette lighter port. She plugged a three-way expansion gadget into the remaining port to make up for the loss. The battery would charge when the bus was running. She connected the inverter and secured it and the battery to the cabinet using a luggage strap. She unpacked the three appliances and stowed them in the cabinet under the sink. She plugged her laptop into the inverter and started it charging. Then she went into the Broken Pony to see how the band was faring.

As she opened the door, she heard the clear, beautiful voice of Cocayne Phillips.

Sometimes you can't forget, and then sometimes you can,
There was a tear of some regret, when the bullet met her
man.

Cocayne hung her head in front of the microphone stand and let the music flow over her, intricate subtle guitar flowing from Link's fingers, Pocket drumming something complicated behind it, supporting it, and blending with Charlie's bass. Sandra didn't move, not wanting to break the spell. *These guys are actually really good.*

Chapter 8: He was Jessica's father, and was as surprised as anyone to find out.

The phone rang. Jack ignored it. It kept ringing until the answering machine took the call. Jack put a pillow over his head, but he could still hear the hushed but urgent tone of the voice on the machine.

"Jack, pick up the phone. Someone's in my apartment and they've cut the power. Get your butt over there and you can nail this guy. Pick up the phone."

He sat up in bed and rubbed his hands over his face, looking at the clock. 2:48 am. *Shit.* The phone clicked. After a moment, it rang again. Jack stood up and felt dizzy, tunnel vision blocking the periphery of his view. He sat back down again. The machine picked up the call.

"Wake up, Jack. The perp is in my house. He's cut the power. He's in my server room. Get your butt out of —"

He had the phone in his hand before she could finish.

"I'm up," he said, the phone to his ear. He listened to the reply.

"I'm going to hang up and call for a patrol car. They can get there a lot faster than I can."

He listened for another moment or two and then put his finger on the receiver hook. He lifted it and called the station.

"This is Jack Morgan. I need patrol cars to the following address," he said and waited for an acknowledgement before reciting the address from memory. "Homicide suspect has broken into the apartment of a witness. Assume he's armed. Secure the building and wait for SWAT. He's probably packing high velocity ammo for a nine millimeter."

Jack pulled on a fresh shirt and picked his pants up off the floor. He dressed quickly, and opened the drawer by the bed, and removed his gun. He had a holster hanging in the closet, but he put the gun into his coat pocket instead. The coat sagged to the left a bit, but it was still more comfortable than wearing a holster in the car.

He called Gonzales.

"Go back to sleep," he said when he got a machine. "I just called SWAT to Millbarque's place. Our guy broke in. You can meet him in the morning."

The phone clicked and Gonzales' voice was loud in his ear. "The hell you say. I'll be there in half an hour."

"See you there," Jack said, and opened the car door, and got in.

At the apartment building, there were two patrol cars with lights flashing, and a SWAT van in the parking lot. Uniformed officers and SWAT unit members in bulletproof vests were standing around or interviewing sleepy apartment dwellers. Jack found the unit leader and introduced himself.

"Power was flipped off at the breaker box," the man said, waving Jack to follow him around the building. "Phones were cut, probably with a cable cutter, looks like a nice neat slice. Entry was on the second floor, empty apartment, sliding glass window on the balcony. He may have had a van parked under it. Some of the bushes are crushed there. We may get tread marks."

"But no suspect," Jack said.

"Place was empty. First officers on the scene saw no vehicle leaving the lot."

Jack was torn between wanting to see the apartment and wanting to see where the suspect entered and left the building. *One thing at a time.* "Let's go see the apartment," he said.

As they walked back towards the front entrance, Jaime Gonzales jogged towards them. "Oh, hi Jacob," he said to the SWAT leader.

"Hey," the man said, not breaking his stride.

"He's gone," Jack said to Gonzales.

"So much for being lucky."

"No, I'm brilliant, remember?" Jack said.

"Right..."

The SWAT team leader slowed, and started veering towards his team and their van.

"Down the hall and on the right," he said. "Unit 31."

"Yeah, we know. Thanks," Jack said. He and Gonzales entered the apartment building.

The door to apartment 31 was propped back up in the broken door frame. A roll of police tape was on the floor. Jack held the doorknob firmly, lifted the door onto the opposite corner, and swung it open, resting it against the wall. The power had been restored, and Jack flipped on the lights.

Nothing looked disturbed in the living room or the kitchen. In the master bedroom, the cell phone was missing, along with the battery that had been lying next to it. In the second bedroom, the computers had been tipped on their sides and opened. Gonzales knelt down to inspect them. "I think he took out the hard drives," he said.

Jack looked over the rest of the room. It was hard to tell if anything else was missing or had been disturbed. This had not been a particularly neat workspace to begin with.

"We're taking these with us," he said to Gonzales, gesturing at the three opened servers on the floor. "I want the guy in IT to look them over. I don't know what to look for."

"There's definitely no hard drives in there," Gonzales said. "They're supposed to be in here, inside this doodad."

"Don't forget who we're dealing with," Jack said.

"Right," Gonzales said. He stood up the first computer and started disconnecting cables.

They carried the computers back out to the parking lot, Gonzales carrying one in each hand, having left the covers back in the apartment. Jack opened the rear of his car and deposited the computer on top of a jacket and baseball cap. Gonzales put the other two next to it, standing them up in order to fit.

"Do you notice anything unusual over there?" Jack said, pointing to a parking space.

Gonzales considered it. "Spot 31 is empty," he said.

"But spot 32 has a Lexus parked in it that wasn't here the first time we paid Mr. Thompson a visit," Jack said.

"That's an awfully nice ride for Mr. Anbar," Gonzales conceded.

"I think we need to pay him a visit," Jack said. He locked up the car, and the two returned to the apartment. Jack spent a minute repositioning the door, and then they knocked on door 32.

Kelly Thompson opened the door. "Hey guys," he said. "You should have been here like an hour ago, these guys came and busted down her door. Scared the crap out of Susie. She took off like a rocket, barely got dressed."

"Does Susie drive a silver Lexus?" Jack asked.

"Huh? No, she rides an old ten-speed. Hell, if she had a car, she could get her own weed."

"Who drives the Lexus?" Jack asked.

"Sandra does," Thompson replied.

"How did it get parked in your parking spot?" Jack prodded.

"Some little Mexican guy. Kept saying 'Hermosa dama' and 'Mujer hermosa', so I know he has the hots for her. I put the keys in the fridge."

"When was this?" Jack asked.

"Before Susie got here," Thompson said. "I was getting the bong all stuffed and straightening up the bed. She hates it when the bed is all wrinkly."

"What time was that?" Jack asked, practicing patience.

"Oh, wow. I don't know. She gets off work at, like, nine o'clock at night, and bikes over here, so it must have been, like, ten or eleven. When she got here, I mean. The Mexican guy was gone by then. He didn't want any weed."

"Was it light or dark outside?" Jack asked.

"When?"

"When the guy dropped off the car," Jack said.

"Dark I think."

"You think," Jack said.

Thompson shrugged. "You guys want some weed?"

"I think we're good," Jack said. "Do you mind if I take the car keys? I'd like to have some people look the car over."

"They're in the fridge," Thompson said.

Jack walked into the kitchen and opened the refrigerator. There were three jars in the door compartment. One still had the prescription. The other was a quarter full of what looked like high-grade marijuana. The third had the keys to the apartment next door and a large electronic key with a Lexus logo. He opened the jar

64

and tipped the car key into his hand. He replaced the jar and closed the door.

Back at the door of Thompson's apartment, he held out his business card. "You call me if you hear anything in the apartment next door, OK?"

"Sure," Thompson said. "But the phone doesn't work."

"They'll get that fixed by morning," Jack said. "You get some sleep."

"You see Susie out there?" Thompson asked.

"I haven't seen her," Jack said. "Or a ten-speed."

"Shit," Thompson said.

Jack nodded and walked out the door. "I know what you mean," he said.

Outside the door, Jack handed the key to Gonzales. "Have fun," he said.

"How come I have to drive it back?" Gonzales asked.

"I have the computers in my car," Jack said.

"You're going to drive me back here to get my car then," Gonzales said.

"How about we pick it up in the morning," Jack said. "Drive the Lexus home. But get the mileage on it first, including the trip odometer. And it'll have GPS, so look for any recent entries. Let's find out where she's been."

Gonzales pushed a button on the key. The silver Lexus chirped, and the interior lights came on.

"Cool," Gonzales said.

Jack nodded and got into his car, suppressing a yawn.

§

Jack was late getting to the station the next morning. He parked next to the silver Lexus that sat where Gonzales usually parked. As he walked towards his desk, he could see chief Wilson, Gonzales, and the fat marshal through the glass wall of the small conference room. He was not looking forward to joining them but turned towards the room anyway.

"You," the marshal said. "Gave me this useless thing." He was waving the DVD again.

"Good morning," Jack said to Wilson and Gonzales.

"Not only does it crash the computer, it's completely unreadable."

"You need the decryption key," Jack said.

"Of course we do. And without that, it's completely useless."

"He was Jessica's father, and was as surprised as anyone to find out," Jack said.

"Who was?" the fat man said, looking puzzled. "Who is Jessica?"

"It's the decryption key," Jack said. "Don't forget to type the apostrophe, the comma, and the period."

"And this Jessica knows how to find the suspect?" the fat man asked.

"There is no Jessica. It's just a password," Jack said.

"Pass phrase," Gonzales said. "They're more secure than passwords. There's a whole thing about them on Wikipedia. We checked it out yesterday."

"It has 68 characters, two of them upper case, three punctuation marks, and it does not occur in any published book or on the Internet. We talked to a computer security guy at Berkeley, and he said that makes it better than military grade as a secure password. Something like 96 bits of what they call entropy. That's a lot." Jack looked over at Wilson, who was trying to figure out if Jack was making all this up.

"You've seen what is on this disk?" the marshal asked.

"Yes," Jack said. "It's a comprehensive list of everything known about the guy who's killing witnesses, and your marshals. It shows what phone numbers he uses, which ones he calls, what kind of ammo he buys, even his favorite brand of Scotch. It tracks his Internet use and what credit cards he uses. It's a gold mine."

"So how come he's not in custody?" the marshal asked belligerently.

Jack paused, and looked at the marshal for a moment before he answered. "Well, you haven't been looking for him for that long. What's it been, 18 months? 20? We almost had him last night, but then we've been looking for him for three whole days now."

"The SWAT thing last night was this guy?" Wilson asked.

"He was in and out in less than 20 minutes," Jack said. "Very professional, he knew exactly how to get in, and exactly what he needed to get. He also knew our response time. The van he used is down in impound. That's where I was a few minutes ago, why I was late. It's clean, stolen from a dry cleaner about a half hour before the break-in. We found it a few blocks away."

"Why wasn't I informed of this?" the marshal asked, getting worked up again.

"That's what this meeting is for," Wilson cut in, before Jack could comment.

Jack pulled a folded piece of paper from his shirt pocket and handed it to the marshal. "You'll want this," he said.

"What is this?" the marshal asked, unfolding the paper.

"It's the pass phrase," Jack said. "My memory isn't all that great. I had to print it out."

After the marshal left, Wilson met Jack and Gonzales at Jack's desk.

"So what did he get?" Wilson asked.

"Cell phone and the hard drives from her computer," Gonzales said.

"We already had the contacts from her phone," Jack said. "We got that in the search. Which means he already had that, since he's been able to read anything on our computers for weeks. So we don't know why he bothered to take the phone."

Gonzales cut in. "He has the disk drives, and he can put them in another computer and try to read them. But my guess is that she has them encrypted like all her other stuff. The guy at Berkeley said that probably only the NSA could read it, and he wasn't sure about them."

"He thought he had us bugged," Jack said. "Maybe he expected us to get the passwords for him."

"He's after the chick," Gonzales said. "He could beat it out of her."

Wilson turned to him. "I thought he wanted the phone and the computers so he could find her."

Gonzales had no answer for that.

Jack paused. "Maybe he's just cleaning up. He thought she might have something on him. He obviously thinks she's a threat."

Wilson pointed his finger at Jack. "Find the guy. Then ask him." He walked out of the room.

Gonzales stood up. "The car was in Sacramento last time someone used the GPS to find out how to get it home."

Jack followed him out the door. "Any of her known associates live in Sacramento?"

Gonzales shook his head. "Her mother has a house in San Diego, but she's in a hospice right now, so the house is empty. She has a sister in L.A., but the car was nowhere near either place. The marshals have guys watching the sister's place, just in case either Millbarque or the suspect show up there."

"The mother's in hospice?"

"Liver cancer. Both sisters were there when she was admitted, but it's down in L.A., and our girl hasn't been there since."

Jack considered this. "The marshals aren't watching the hospice?"

Gonzales shook his head. "Manpower. The place is cooperating, and they're supposed to be giving the marshals a call about any visitors."

Jack didn't like that. "Sounds to me like they're watching the wrong place. If your mom was dying, wouldn't you pay her a visit? Even if you were on the lam?"

"If our guy thinks like you do, he's probably headed that way," Gonzales said.

Jack sat down at his desk. "The guy hires private detectives," he said. "We should see if he has eyes on the place."

68

The two worked through lunch, making phone calls and using the computer, and eating sandwiches Jimmy Wallace had brought back from the local deli.

Chapter 9: He was so polite over tea that she almost regretted the arsenic.

Link drove the bus back to the Broken Pony after lunch. Sandra and the rest of the band sat on the two couches, cracking jokes at one another's expense. Lunch had been great, and Sandra had her Internet connection, and life was good. She could hardly wait until the band resumed practice, so she could be alone in the bus with her computer. She was dying to find out what had happened last night.

They seemed to take forever to set back up, but once they were on the stage, they forgot about Sandra, and she quietly slipped out the door into the afternoon heat. There was a slight breeze, and all the bus windows were open, but it was still hot inside. She turned on the computer, connected to the new router, and set up a privacy proxy server connection to Portugal.

She called Jack Morgan. He answered on the first ring.

"Morgan."

"How did it go last night?"

"Well, if it isn't my favorite fugitive from justice." Jack seemed pleased with himself.

"You caught him!"

"I'm afraid not. He was in and out. He knew our response time, and he'd cased the place thoroughly."

"Shit."

"Yeah. What does he want with your hard drives?" Jack asked.

"Anything he can learn about me."

"I assume they were protected?" Jack asked.

Apparently, he hadn't examined them during the search. "Shit no, they're honeypots."

There was a pause. "What are they?"

"Honeypots. Traps. They are set up to record any traffic that goes to them and send alerts. I set up breadcrumbs, so the victim will be attracted to the web sites on the server. If someone falls for it, I learn a little more about them. Suppose I put up some comments on well-trafficked web sites, saying something like 'I got this weird call from someone at (202) 456-1414.' And I make it look like my comment came from the honeypot server. If the target sees the message and pokes around the server, then I know

70

he at least Googled for his phone number, or credit card number, or whatever the bait was. Maybe I'm using a license plate number, or an address, or something. Anything that only my target will really be interested in."

Jack took this in.

"So what could he learn from your drives?"

"He might have just fallen for the honeypot. If he figures that out, then he'd want to erase his tracks. But he could learn a lot about me and my methods by studying what's on those drives."

"Such as?"

"Like how not to fall for any honeypots I set up in the future. Like how my honeypots report what they find. But this guy isn't that smart. He's the guy who kills people. He hires people like Scott to do the stuff that takes brains. If you look for someone hiring people that can analyze stolen drives, you might find him. You're working with the marshals. Have them ask their FBI buddies to search the black hat networks for people bidding on that."

"What about the marshals?"

"Jack, you know I can do my job. And I know you're very good at your job. Of course, you have the marshals in on this. They've been at this guy for two years. So don't play stupid with me. If you weren't a real smart cookie, you wouldn't be where you are, and I wouldn't be working with you."

Jack was silent. Then he asked, "How is Sacramento?"

"Hot. How's my car? Did the little guy take good care of it?"

"What little guy would that be?" Jack asked.

"You're good at this game," Sandra said. "But Kelly would have told you all about him. I'm glad he got away."

"Nice trick with CleanSweep," Jack said.

"At least you're protected now. How did the sweep for bugs go?"

"What's that?" Jack asked.

"You wouldn't have brought up CleanSweep if it hadn't found something. So you must have swept for listening devices after that, and you're speaking freely about details of the case, so you must have found and removed those too."

There was a pause. Just a slight one, but Sandra knew what it meant. She filled in quickly.

"So, you found the note I left for you in the car, then?" As she spoke, she was quickly bringing up her email.

"Sandy, that was so sweet of you," Jack said. He was a quick study after all.

"If you want the rest of it, meet me at the Hilton here in Sacto. Ask the desk for Delia Santiago."

"I think I should write that down," he said. "Delia Santiago, Sacramento Hilton, ask at the desk."

"But not before tomorrow morning at about ten, I haven't checked in yet."

"Tomorrow at ten. Got it," Jack said.

"Ok," Sandra said. "I gotta go." She disconnected.

She emailed Jack Morgan.

Nice save, he'll never fall for it, but it was worth a shot.

Call Jeff Worthington to do the sweep. You can have your guys do one too, but you can trust Jeff to do a better job.

I'm going to set us up a more secure communications channel. You'll know it when you see it.

Trust CleanSweep, but don't trust anything else.

Bring your computer to a park bench somewhere, and use a public WiFi connection.

CleanSweep will make sure it's secure. Don't use the same location twice.

She sent the email.

There was a lot of new email she had not had a chance to read. She quickly disposed of newsletters, digests of interest groups, and other non-critical stuff. The note from her sister had to be read, but not right now. But one subject line caught her attention.

Subject: Hey girlfriend, gone all Black Hat on us? You made the list.

It was from Balrog, one of the people she used for certain hard-to-manage and maybe legal, maybe not kinds of help. It was encrypted and digitally signed. She entered her pass phrase.

Your name popped up on the federal fugitive list.

Just to let you know, I watch out for my friends.

I have 300-odd sniffers on the backbone if you need to do some stochastic modeling.

And JersyGrrl's botnet is still available to us while she's a guest of the state.

Sandra thought carefully about her reply.

Thanks, I may want to take you up on that, but not right now.

I have a package in storage at House of Pain.

Too bad about JersyGrrl, she told me about the key thing.

He was so polite over tea that she almost regretted the arsenic.

She sent it off. At least Balrog would have the data on the client and could add his resources to the hunt.

There was an email from Sharon Tremain. Sandra opened it with a little bit of anxiety. What was Scott's wife going to say to his suddenly missing business associate?

I hope you're OK, and far away from here. You must know about Scott by now. Whatever they were looking for in the office, they didn't find it, and I don't know what it might have been, but someone was prowling around here last night. They left in a hurry when we turned on the lights, and I didn't get a good look. Scott said the two of you were onto something big, and not to trust the police if they came around. He said you were the only one to trust. I hope this gets to you.

Sandra took a deep breath and closed her eyes. The rest of the email could wait.

She set up a GMail account for *detective.jack.morgan @ gmail.com* and started building a security package for him.

It was hard to finish. The tears were making it hard to see the screen. *Scott, I'm so sorry.*

She closed the laptop and folded her arms on the table, her head down on her shirtsleeves, and let the tears come.

§

Sandra didn't hear anyone get on the bus, but she lifted her head when Cocayne sat down on the bench seat across the table.

"I can leave," Cocayne said, seeing the tears on Sandra's face.

"No, that's all right," Sandra said and wiped her face with her sleeve. "I'm just trying to keep too many balls in the air, trying not to think about bad things happening to good people."

"Your ex?" Cocayne asked.

"No. My mom is dying. The guy I work for just died, and I couldn't do anything. It's just, damn," she said, wiping her face again.

Cocayne took her hand. "You sure keep a lot bottled up, girl," she said.

"I have to be really careful," Sandra said. "I have to be someone else now. I have to break all ties with who I was last week, or else..."

"Or else what?" Cocayne asked softly.

"I'm in trouble," Sandra said. "Someone is looking for me, and they are very good at what they do. I'm very good at it too, and that scares me to death, because I know all the ways you can fuck it up."

"Your ex, the cop."

"No, he's not really my ex. He is a cop, though. I didn't do anything, he's not trying to put me in jail or anything, but he's looking for me, and the other guy who's looking for me knows that and can use that to find me, and he's the one that really scares me. Shit, it's complicated, and I really can't tell anyone about it, it just makes people make mistakes, that's how people get caught."

Cocayne sat quietly, holding Sandra's hand.

"How can we help?" she asked after a few minutes of thought.

Sandra looked up at her. "You guys have already been a great help," she said. "Who would expect to look for me here?"

Cocayne looked out the window. "It *is* kind of a shithole," she said.

"That's not what I meant," Sandra said. "But I already fucked it up, using my real name. I need a new name. Something random."

"Jane Random," Cocayne said. "Does it have to be boring?"

74

"In my business, I use statistics to model people and their activities," Sandra said. "People are predictable if you have enough data. They can't actually make random choices. They always give something away. You can't just pick a name, for example. I might run a sim and find out that you pick names for your pets that start with S, or that you like three syllables, or whatever. It doesn't have to be a lot, but combined with everything else I know about you, it can help narrow the search down to a small enough number that I can start fishing, sending emails to all the targets, or calling numbers with a robodialer and asking innocent-sounding questions. So, the only way to really be safe is to use dice or something, to get real random choices."

"We don't have any dice," Cocayne said.

"I sometimes use license plate numbers. Like flipping a coin. The next license plate number I see is either odd or even, like heads or tails."

Cocayne took that in. Then she stood up. "Cool. Let's go get you a name."

She held out her hand to Sandra and pulled her up off the bench seat. They got off the bus and Cocayne led them out to the street. They waited in the hot sun for a car to drive by.

"305 TJD," Cocayne read as a red pickup truck breezed by.

"So, I'm 305," Sandra said, grinning at the younger woman. "Just call me 3 for short."

"You're my good friend T.J.," Cocayne said. "Charlie Daniels' favorite sister."

"The T. can't be for Theresa," Sandra said.

"You sure as fuck aren't a Tiffany or a Tammy," Cocayne said.

"I can't pick the name," Sandra said. "It has to be totally random, or you have to pick it."

"You go by T.J.," Cocayne said, "because the initials stand for something so awful you won't let anyone know what they are."

"Like Tiffany or Tammy," Sandra said.

"Worse. Tabitha. Tabitha Jean. No that has a nice rhythm. Tabitha Jessica. Tabitha Jessica Daniels. That is just awful, I can see why you go by TJ."

"You're having fun with this," Sandra said.

Cocayne drew her close, and put her hand on Sandra's shoulder. "Not a word of this, or I rip your lips off, you hear? But my mother named me Cokie. And I have yet to forgive her for that."

Sandra put her hand on the smaller woman's shoulder and said seriously, "And nobody calls me Tabitha and lives."

"Damn right," Cocayne said, and they broke into giggles. "Come on, TJ, let me introduce you to the band."

§

Inside the Broken Pony, Link was on stage alone. His guitar hung from his shoulder strap as he adjusted the bass and treble controls. Then he stood up straight, closed his eyes, and began to play. The melody was intricate, with an unusual rhythm, almost stumbling but catching itself just in time on each measure. The effect was hypnotic and fascinating, punctuated by surprising turns that kept bringing the melody back to the central theme in different ways. The chorus broke into a fast-paced, exciting rocket of notes and then blended smoothly back into the verse by simply eliminating every other beat.

The newly minted TJ Daniels was spellbound until the solo completed, and Link bent down to adjust something by the foot pedals.

"I keep telling you, Link, I can't write lyrics to shit in 5/4 time," Cocayne called up to him, sitting down at a round table in the back of the room. She turned to Sandra/TJ. "He loves stuff like Brubeck's *Take Five*, or the *Mission Impossible* music. Says if Al Jarreau can write words to it, then I should be able to."

Pocket put his hands on her shoulders, leaning over from behind her. "And that shit is a real bitch to drum to," he said. "All your instincts want to cut the first two beats in half and make it 4/4. Like Jethro Tull's *Living in the Past*, or Sting's *Seven Days*."

"But it's so beautiful," Sandra said.

"Instrumentals don't sell," Cocayne said.

Link tapped on a microphone. "I've been working on something," he said and started to play again. It was the same melody. But Link started to sing along.

Got a five-leg dog,

The guitar played another bar alone, letting the words sink in.

He don't walk too well.

Again, the guitar took the next verse, as if in response.

Got a fun-ny gait,

...

Likes to sit and wait.

...

But we have our fun,

...

'Cause he LOVES to RUN!

The guitar took off, and Sandra could picture a dog running free and fast, five beats and a leap, five and a leap, fluid and smooth.

Hold him still until you say go,
He'll be back before the echo.
We will always be together,
Love to watch him run forever.

Pocket jumped up on the stage and sat down behind the drum kit, and Charlie followed, picking up his bass. Tentatively, Pocket started marking beats, just little taps on the cymbals. Charlie thumped the bass on the first beat of each measure, feeling his way into the music.

"I gotta say," Cocayne said to Sandra, "he's made it work, but it's only half a song. There's no metaphor yet, no kick in the pants, make you think, pull you off the floor finish to it." She got up and joined the band on the stage, nodding her head with the beat. She took the microphone.

If you think you're strange,
Can't quite make it right,
Like it's never been,
Yours to fit right in,
When you hear the gun,
Just get UP and RUN!

Don't hold back until you get there,
Let them talk 'cause what do you care,
Show them all there's nothing to it,
We were born to ride right through it.

The song continued with the first verse again, Cocayne and Link singing together, and stopped suddenly on the shouted *RUN!*

"Well, shit," Cocayne said. "That sure needs work."

"But you found the hook," Link said.

"You gave me a five-legged dog, for chrissake!" Cocayne said. "What else could I do but work the alienation angle? We don't do cute. Nobody comes to a *Full Auto* show to come out cooing 'Aw, he's da widdo puppy.' We want them pumped!"

78

Pocket pulled a microphone to his lips. "At least she didn't kill the poor little thing," he said.

"That would have spiced it up, eh?" Cocayne said. "Maybe I should work on that."

Sandra walked up to sit on the edge of the stage.

"Is that how you write the songs?" she asked. "You make it look so easy."

Cocayne laughed. "Link, how long have you been working on that? Since Tucson?" She turned to Sandra. "That thing won't be ready for real people to hear it for months, and when it's done, it won't be anything like the rot you just heard. He's got the music tight, but come on, a five-legged dog?"

"It's five four time, see," Link began.

"She gets it," Cocayne said. "Just because she liked it doesn't mean she's an idiot." She looked at Sandra. "Or maybe not."

Pocket threw a drumstick at her back.

§

When eight o'clock came around, there were perhaps a dozen people in line to get in. The band started with an energetic first set, trying to work up some enthusiasm in the crowd, but there just weren't enough people in the room. No one sat in the tables close to the band, except for Sandra, who thought that maybe she was keeping people at bay somehow.

She watched the door, and in the next half hour, only two more couples entered the room. Cocayne tried to engage the audience by aiming her voice at particular tables, but it seemed to have no effect. The band had started a slow ballad when a man came to Sandra's table and asked, "Is this seat taken?"

"Not at all," she said, gesturing towards the chair next to hers, facing the band. He took the seat.

He looked like he might be a local, so Sandra asked him, "Is it just Wednesday night, or is it usually this slow?"

He shook his head. "I think everybody is at the Jessie Carter concert at the Pavilion," he said. "It's held over, and they put more tickets on sale. It's kind of too bad. That crowd would probably really like this band. Cerebral," he said, tapping his temple.

She nodded, listening to the music.

"Not a lot of advertising," the man said. "I didn't know who would be here until I drove past the sign."

She nodded again. Was this guy just trying to pick up the only single woman in the room? She looked around. There were two tables that had odd numbers of women. She wasn't the only potential target. The word sent a chill to the back of her neck. Who was this guy?

"So, what do you do?" he asked.

"Real estate," she said, using the cover she had arranged. Too bad it hadn't been insurance sales. That would send him packing.

"In Las Vegas, in this economy? That must be like unemployed," he said.

"Seattle," she said. Maybe he'd get the idea if she gave one-word answers.

"I'm getting a drink," he said. "Can I get you something?"

She shook her head and pointed to the glass of ice water in front of her. It had a lime in it. It could be a drink, as far as he could tell.

He left the table. Where could she have gone wrong? If this was someone looking for her, had they found Rafael, and had he told them about the band? How many people might be looking for her? Federal marshals, Jack Morgan, the client and any investigators he might have hired, and maybe someone who had hired the client had also put the word out. She imagined her picture, and a photo of the *Full Auto* bus, and their itinerary. And the ad in Ridester, with her real name, and the list of people who had looked at that ad. Cocayne had probably used her phone to view it. *I could track that phone. That means he could.*

Could they have put it together in just three days? Could she have? Jack knew she had been in Sacramento. That meant the client knew. In Sacramento without a car. Check the cabs, the airport, and the buses. Did they have access to the Ridester database? That would take a while, and a bit of social engineering. Or a subpoena. If the police or the marshals had thought to look there, the client would have the information.

I could leave. Go out to the bus, and see if he followed.

Great idea. Then she'd be alone in the bus, with a killer right on her tail.

I need a date.

She looked around the room, and spotted two young men holding beers and standing near the back wall. She stood up, glancing at the bar where the man was still waiting for his drink, and walked over to the two men.

"I love this band," she said, shouting over the music. She positioned herself so she could see the bar in her peripheral vision.

"Never heard of them before," said the taller of the two.

"What kind of music is that?" said the other.

Sandra made an exaggerated shrug. "I don't know, but I love it!"

They nodded. The man left the bar with his drink, looking around. She looked away.

"You live around here?" she asked.

"Spring Valley," the taller one said.

"UNLV," the other one said.

No wonder they look so young. She felt suddenly uncomfortable. They would not be interested in some woman ten years older. *Do the math, girl, almost 20 years older.*

She didn't want to date them. She just needed them for cover. She scanned the room, looking for the man who had selected her from the crowd. She relaxed. He was hitting on one of the women at the bar.

Paranoia might keep her safe, but it sure was a bitch.

"I was thinking of teaching there," she said to the shorter man. "Calculus and statistics."

Neither one of them had a reply for that. After a while, the taller one spoke up. "I'm getting another beer," he said.

"Me too," the shorter one said and waved at Sandra.

She smiled. Can't make them come, but I can sure make them go.

She went out to the bus and unlocked the door, getting her laptop off of the table in the rear. She brought it back into the Broken Pony, and found an unoccupied table in the rear of the club, and sat down with her back against the wall.

It was time to send Jack the security package.

Chapter 10: As last thoughts go, wishing you had loaded your gun was a good one.

Jack's phone rang.

"Morgan," he said, and listened for a reply.

"Well, if it isn't my favorite fugitive from justice," he said cheerfully.

Gonzales listened as the two played cat and mouse on the phone.

"How is Sacramento?" Jack asked. If she denied being there, then she was probably still there.

"What little guy would that be?" Gonzales could almost follow the conversation.

"Nice trick with the CleanSweep." Jack was smiling at Gonzales, obviously enjoying playing games with the clever woman.

"What's that?" Jack's face was suddenly deadly serious, and Gonzales picked up the headphones to listen in.

"...so, you must have removed those too," he heard her say.

Jack was looking around his desk, at the phone, at the computer.

"So, you found the note I left for you in the car, then?" Gonzales heard Sandra say in the headphones.

Jack held his finger to his lips and shot Gonzales a worried look.

"Sandy," he said. "That was so sweet of you." He dripped sarcasm in an attempt to make the comment fit in with the previous conversation.

"If you want the rest of it, meet me at the Hilton here in Sacto. Ask the desk for Delia Santiago."

"I think I should write that down," Jack said. "Delia Santiago, Sacramento Hilton, ask at the desk."

"But not before tomorrow morning at about ten, I haven't checked in yet."

"Tomorrow at ten. Got it," Jack said.

"Ok," Gonzales heard. "I gotta go." The phone disconnected.

Jack stood up quickly and held his finger to his lips again, gesturing Gonzales to follow him.

83

He stopped when his computer beeped, and he saw Sandra's email come in. He picked up the computer, and the two men walked out of the building, Jack reading the email as they strode out the door towards Jack's car.

"The guy's got the office bugged," Jack said.

"No way," Gonzales said.

"She's been right about this guy every time so far. She knows how he works. Until we know the station is clean, we can't talk about the case. Not there. We have to find someplace else for meetings."

Jack opened the door of his car and sat down sideways in the driver's seat, his feet on the doorsill, his knees supporting the laptop. "What's the damned IT guy's name? Drake, something Drake."

"Larry," Gonzales said.

Jack started an email to Larry Drake, asking him to sweep his office for listening devices.

"Does IT do that?" Gonzales said, trying to read the laptop.

"Who else would you ask?" Jack said. He added to the email, telling Drake to figure out how to do it if the department didn't normally provide those services.

Jack opened Sandra's email again and got out his phone. He did a web search for Jeff Worthington while Gonzales bent over to read the laptop upside-down.

"She just happens to know a guy that sweeps for bugs?" Gonzales asked. "What if she's just playing you, to get more time to get away from Sacramento?"

Jack pointed to the screen. Jeff Worthington: EyeSpy Electronics.

Gonzales squatted to read the screen right side up. "She just happens to know a guy that sweeps for bugs. Who is this chick?"

Jack placed the call.

§

Jeff Worthington was a tall, thin man, with a huge reddish-yellow mustache and a stiff, white cowboy hat that looked like he got it at Toys R Us. He was carrying a large black duffle bag that clanked as he moved. It looked heavy, and lumpy.

"Normally I'd have one of my guys come out and do this, but I never got a call from the police before, not for help anyways."

"We appreciate you coming out," Jack said.

"Sandra sent me an email about two minutes after you called," Worthington said. "That's what clinched the deal for me. I mighta blowed you guys off, but you don't pass up an opportunity to get that girl owing you a favor, no way Jose, nosirree. Like money in the bank."

Jack looked over at Gonzales. "You've worked with her before?"

"Girl's got magic fingers. Give her a keyboard and stand back."

"What kind of work does she do?" Jack asked.

Worthington looked at Jack and shifted the big bag on his shoulder. "Let's get this thing done, whataya say?"

The three men left Worthington's van parked next to Jack's car and walked into the police station.

None of them said a word as Worthington set the bag on Jack's desk with a clatter as hidden metal boxes rearranged themselves inside. He unzipped the bag and searched inside for the particular box he wanted. He found it, and pulled it out of the bag, and slid a switch to turn it on. Then he removed the cord from the phone and plugged it into the box.

He went back to the bag and selected another box. He removed the telephone handset and plugged that into the second box. He switched the box on, and a light started flashing.

Worthington looked up at Jack, and pointed at the telephone receiver, and nodded, wagging his finger disapprovingly at the offending phone.

Another box came out of the bag. It was more complicated, with a stubby antenna and an LCD display. Worthington turned it on and entered some numbers on its keypad. He waved the device around the desk and up and down the sides of the desk, staring at the readout. He opened desk drawers and waved the device inside them, taking items out of the drawers and putting them onto the desk. Jack's calculator, a pen, a digital voice recorder, and an LED flashlight all came out and were placed on the desk.

More boxes came out of the bag and were used in turn. More items joined the pile on the desk. Office supplies in their unopened boxes, and the box the calculator had come in, with its instruction manual inside.

Worthington took out the largest item in the bag: a cube with two meters on the front, some adjusting dials, and four stubby antennas on the top, arranged in a square, one near each corner. There was a circle of red LEDs between the antennas. He turned it on, and held it in front of his large belt buckle, and started turning around, watching the lights. No matter which way he turned, the light nearest the east wall of the station lit up.

He tipped his head towards the door, and Jack and Gonzales followed him outside.

"There's one in the phone for sure. Short range, so there's a repeater somewhere nearby. It's probably wired, or I would have picked up the signal. Or maybe there's a high gain antenna within a few hundred feet of here aimed at your office. But the really interesting part is the microwave beam."

Jack looked at him and then at Gonzales to see if the other man had any more insight into what was just said than he had.

"There's a microwave transmitter over in that direction," Worthington said, waving his hand east. "Like a WiFi transmitter or a cordless phone, but stronger, and directional, and unmodulated. That means there's no signal on it. It goes through the building, and I expect there's a receiver somewhere on the other side, over there somewhere," he said, waving his hand to the west.

"By the time the signal gets there, though, it's modulated. A little bit of wire, a printed circuit, actually, probably hidden under some tape, is attached to something that vibrates with sound, like a cardboard box, or the bottom of a desk drawer. That wiggles the printed circuit, which was designed to resonate at the same frequency as the microwave beam. It acts like a passive microphone."

"We can get rid of them then," Jack said.

"Oh sure, if that's what you want to do," Worthington said. "Wouldn't you rather catch the guy who's listening?"

The three men talked in the parking lot for another hour, discussing details, planning, and estimating the odds of success of each approach. Then they went back to collect Worthington's equipment from Jack's desk and brought it back to the van.

"One more thing," Worthington said, pulling a box from the van and opening it. "Sandra said to give you a couple of these. She said they were for someone named Delia. She said you'd know what that meant."

He held out two cell phones with large screens and two small black buttons. "These have little magnets, so you can stick the little suckers wherever you like," he said, putting one of the buttons against the side of the van. It stuck, as advertised. He turned on one of the cell phones, and Jack could see himself in the display.

"The cameras have a range of about 300 feet, so you have to stay pretty close. But the receivers can record about 3 hours of the video, if you don't want to watch it in real time. The batteries in the cameras won't last that long, though, maybe an hour. But they turn on only when the receiver is on, so you can save the batteries until they're needed."

Jack held the screen up and turned around in front of the camera, looking at the back of his head.

"I'll be wanting those back soon," Worthington said. "Little suckers cost an arm and a leg."

They watched the van drive away, and Gonzales turned to Jack. "This is getting fucking weird."

Gonzales left in his car, and Jack went back into the building.

Wilson was careful about how he spoke while in the bugged station.

"Don't the marshals have someone in Sacramento they can send?" Wilson wanted to know.

"Sure," Jack said. "But she's not going to just turn herself in to a federal marshal. If she wanted to do that, she could have done it any time. She's got the goods on this guy, and she only trusts me with the disk. I promised not to bring her in if she handed it over. She won't deal with anyone else."

"And you think what she has is worth a round trip to Sacramento," Wilson said.

"She's convinced it's enough to nail him. And connect him to other murders besides Tremain."

"Pack your bags, then. I'm authorizing it," Wilson said.

The two men walked out of the building together.

"You think he was listening to all of that?" Wilson asked.

"The guy can't be everywhere at once. I can't believe he could get a licensed investigator to bug a police station, so that part he either did himself or contracted out to someone who is not averse to breaking the law on a routine basis. But we can't know how many people he has working for him. Contract killing can't be that lucrative. There are so many amateurs out there who will work for peanuts." Jack stopped at his car.

"Something like this could be personal, worth it to someone to do it right. The cleanup part, Tremain and the Millbarque woman, that part could just be the contractor screwing up. Like he planned on it ending with Tremain."

"Or he just didn't count on Millbarque being as good as she is," Jack said. "But something about this says it's bigger than that to me. Something the marshals aren't telling us."

"Don't underestimate Laurel and Hardy," Wilson said. "The fat guy is an ass, but the skinny guy that keeps his mouth shut and lets the fat guy make an ass of himself, scuttlebutt has it that guy is a sharp cookie."

"Too bad the fat guy does all the talking," Jack said.

Wilson looked at his watch. "Gonzales must be halfway to Sacramento about now."

"Hilton security has a room for him for tonight. He'll have the toys in place and the staff briefed. A security guy will be doing the actual front desk duty from nine to noon tomorrow."

"Have a nice flight," Wilson said.

§

88

Jack went over his notes on the computer, sitting at the table in the kitchen. He thought about how he would handle the encounter in the morning in Sacramento. The suspect was most likely armed. He liked high-power nine-millimeter ammunition. He'd be concealing it under a jacket or sport coat, in the Sacramento heat. That was not the kind of gun you'd wear on an ankle holster.

He'd be muscular. Strong enough to strangle a man with a wire garrote and not move his feet in the blood spatter.

Gonzales would be watching over video, out of sight. That meant Gonzales would not be able to fire on the suspect if he pulled a gun on Jack. Jack would have his gun in his coat pocket and would have it always pointed at the suspect, without alarming the others in the room.

He'd be loitering at the counter for some reason. Maybe filling out a job application, or something else that would take some time. He'd have to do that left-handed, so his right hand would stay in his pocket. He could not be wearing his badge on his belt. It would have to be concealed, probably in the other coat pocket, or the inside pocket.

What do you say when you arrest a contract killer? How would he react to "You're under arrest"?

Tell him exactly what to do, so he doesn't think of doing what you don't want him to do. Hands on the counter. Feet back. Disarm him yourself, or keep a gun on him while a partner takes his weapons? The textbooks are written to cover the common cases, protecting the suspect as much as the officer. What would you change if you were dealing with someone used to killing for a living, and who had everything to lose if he got caught?

Because this guy was going to die if he got caught, one way or another. If his employers didn't get to him before the trial, they would get to him during or after it. These were people who could find witnesses under protection and kill them without a second thought.

Of course, he might not show up. Probably wouldn't show up. But if he did, you had to be very well prepared. He got his gun out of the locked drawer and put an extra magazine into his suitcase.

As last thoughts go, wishing you had loaded your gun was a good one.

It was getting quite late, but he checked his email one last time.

There was an email from detective.jack.morgan@gmail.com. He considered whether to open it, but curiosity got the better of him. It was from Millbarque.

I've put together a security package for you.

It will allow you to digitally sign your correspondence and encrypt it, and allow us to communicate and know we are talking to the right person, and not some impersonator.

Normally the problem with digital signatures is establishing a chain of trust. If I handed you a key in person, you could then trust that only I could sign something with that key. But a key is not something that I can send you in an email. So, I built the next best thing. In the attached package is a program that uses video as a passphrase. Play the video that accompanies it, and if you are sure that only I could send you that, then run the attached program. Then we can set up a video chat session, and use the video of that session as our passphrase.

There were two items attached. One was a file called rename_me_foo_dot_exe, and the other was a video file. Jack clicked on the video, and it began to play.

He saw himself enter Millbarque's apartment and pick up the phone. The video ended at that point.

He smiled. It *did* seem unlikely that anyone else would have had that video.

He clicked on the attachment, and his computer told him it did not know what to do with the file.

He renamed the file *foo.exe* and tried again. It ran, and a green bar in a box slowly grew longer until it reached 100%.

A window popped up on his screen after less than a minute, and a face appeared in it.

"I really didn't expect you to be up this late, Jack," the face said.

"Me either," Jack said. "Your driver's license photo does not do you justice." He could hear music in the background. Her face seemed to be lit mainly from her computer screen.

"You say that to all the girls," she said. "That should be enough video to establish the signature. The security package contains programs for sending email, making telephone calls, and this video chat program. If you use those, then all of our communications will be encrypted and routed through anonymizing servers at random around the world, and everything will be digitally signed."

Jack nodded. Millbarque continued.

"There are two passphrases listed in the secure directory. Pick one you think you can memorize. I tried to make them hard to forget. If you want to let me know you are under duress, or think someone is watching over your shoulder or listening in, then don't capitalize the first letter."

"You really don't trust anyone, do you?" Jack asked.

"I'm trusting you," she said. "And now I will be able to know it really is you."

"If he's at the Hilton tomorrow, this will all be over," Jack said.

"Let's hope he's there," she said. "But it won't be over until we find who he's working for."

"I saw your notes on that."

"I'm still working on it. I have some friends helping me out. They have methods I don't normally condone, but this is a special case," she said.

"Let's hope they have better luck than we've been having at this end," Jack said.

"Be really careful tomorrow," Millbarque said, her face showing real concern. "This is not a nice guy."

He smiled. "You be careful too."

She winked. "Always."

The screen went dark. Jack closed the computer and sat back in the chair. It was really going to be hard to get any sleep tonight.

Chapter 11: She took one last deep breath and wished she had learned how to swim.

Sandra hadn't heard the band get back on the bus the night before. She had been very soundly asleep. In the morning, she tried to be as quiet as possible, so as not to wake them. She carried her computer out behind the Broken Pony and found a comfortable place to sit: her back against a small tree; her feet in a small patch of well-tended grass. She hoped the sprinklers didn't have this time of day in mind to do some watering.

The sun had not yet risen above the buildings, but the crisp cold of the desert night had already faded, and the lack of wind promised another scorching day. But for now, the morning was quite pleasant, and she got down to work.

Her *DIY Witness Protection* book was a little long for an eBook, coming in at 30 pages, and she had a lot more to say, but that could be put in the website content, and in the blog. Giving away free information was the best way to get people to buy an online book.

She set up an account with ClickBank for Xavier Hargrove. His address in Wellington, courtesy of privatebox.co.nz, would get the printed checks. People could now buy the book using ClickBank, and PrivateBox would mail the checks to the lawyer in Sacramento. That lawyer had set up a fictitious business name statement filing in Sacramento, saying that she was doing business as Xavier Dylan Hargrove. The lawyer would cash the checks, and she would let him know where to send the money. A box full of twenty-dollar bills could arrive for TJ Daniels at the Broken Pony, or whatever venue the band was playing at the time.

Thanks to automated Twitter software, Xavier already had more followers on Twitter than the real Sandra had ever had. Anyone tweeting about computer security in the form of several keywords had been automatically followed, and most of those people had followed back. Xavier tweeted that he had a new website up, and a new eBook with some clever security tricks for staying private while making a living on the Internet.

She used one of her pre-paid gift cards to place some ads for the site. She added affiliate links to the website to sell other

92

people's software through ClickBank and get part of the profit for her marketing efforts.

With luck, Jack Morgan would catch the guy at the Hilton and all of this would just be a nice exercise. But if this lifestyle had to be kept up for months, it would be nice to have some money coming in.

"There you are," Cocayne said from behind her. She cleared the screen with a quick key sequence and turned her head to look around the tree.

"This is nice," Cocayne said, coming around to sit on the grass in front of Sandra.

"What time did you guys get to bed last night?" Sandra asked.

"I'm sure it was morning," Cocayne said. "I swear to you, we normally get a lot more people at a gig than that."

"What kind of advertising do you do?"

"Us? No, the club does all that stuff," Cocayne said.

Sandra brought up a browser and looked up the Broken Pony. Cocayne crab-walked over to see the screen as she typed. "Live bands daily," Sandra read aloud. She looked up *Full Auto*, but there was nothing in the first 100 links that had anything to do with the band.

She looked over at Cocayne. "You know, I know a lot about how to generate traffic to a web site. And I'll bet we can do a lot better than the Broken Pony has been doing as far as local advertising goes. How about we play a few games and see if we can get a crowd worked up?"

She got out her gift card again. "First, we set up some online ads. One trick we can use is really dead simple and cheap. You put everything the person needs to know in the ad, so there's no need for them to click on it. No clicks, no cost. We can then offer to pay a dollar a click, and get top billing."

She set up some ads for "henderson night club" and "henderson live band" and quickly added a dozen more that were similar, using keyword suggestions from the advertising web page. The content of the ad had the name of the club, their phone number, and address, and "*Full Auto* band held over due to overwhelming demand!"

"Wait a minute," Cocayne said. "That's not even remotely true."

"And scrubbing bubbles don't smile and push little brushes around your toilet, either. It's an ad. Everybody lies in ads. Do you have samples of your music on the web site?"

"You mean for free?" Cocayne asked.

"I'll take that as a no," Sandra said. "We'll fix that later. Go get me a CD or an MP3 with your best songs on it, and I'll set up a couple blogs while you're doing that."

Cocayne got up, and Sandra had set up four new blogs at free sites by the time she came back. Cocayne handed her the CD, and she put it into the computer, then picked four of her favorite songs and copied them to the blogs.

"We saw this *totally killer* band last night at the Broken Pony. Awesome. Completely awesome. I just had to snag their CD. This track had everybody rocking, I thought the walls were going to come down."

She made three more entries that were similar, and then commented on them under different names, all in complete agreement with the original post. Then she started searching for blogs and portals for local Henderson nightlife and pasted those comments in as many places as she could.

"Now we need to find out what the local little newspapers are. You know, the little free ones that have all the real estate ads and stuff. People check those out when they want to know who's playing where." Sandra's fingers worked quickly. She found what she was looking for.

"Want to go talk to a newspaper reporter?" she asked.

"Me?"

"Yes, lead singer of the band, cool name, they'll love you. I'll call a cab. If we take the motorcycle, we'll both look like shit when we get there." She got the CD out of the computer. "We'll want this. And bring your MP3 player, they might not want to play the CD on their computer."

§

"You bring a friend today?" the cab driver asked.

"Rajiv, this is Ms. Phillips. She's the lead singer of a famous touring group, and we're keeping a low profile, so no first names, OK? The band is playing small venues to test new material, and the Broken Pony is their latest stop."

The cab driver stared at Cocayne, trying to guess which famous singer she was.

"Ms. Phillips, this is my friend Rajiv," Sandra continued. "I gave him a thorough test run yesterday. He can be trusted."

"Charmed," Cocayne said, extending her hand. Rajiv shook her hand awkwardly, twisting around in the seat.

Rajiv talked all the way to the newspaper office, and the topic seemed to change every 20 seconds. Cocayne and Sandra whispered to one another in the back seat.

"You know this guy?"

"I asked for his business card yesterday," Sandra said. "If you don't want to be found, use the same cab all the time. The fewer people you deal with, the lower the chance one of them will spill some dangerous information about you. On the other hand, if you want people to find you, tell a cabbie you're famous. The word will get all around town in no time."

"How do you know all this stuff?"

"It's my job to find people," Sandra said. "That gives me some insight into how to hide, and how to be found. I've just never been on this side of things before. And trying to hide and be found at the same time is kind of confusing. I'm still working through some of the details."

"But you're not trying to be found," Cocayne said.

"Trying to make my travelling companions get a lot of attention is not that far off from being found. The good news is, when I'm with you, everyone looks at you. The bigger I can make your shadow, the easier it will be to hide in it. At least, I hope. It's like a magician making you look at the hand that *doesn't* have the coin in it."

Cocayne sat a little straighter in the seat. "Well then, I'm just going to have to get my diva on, won't I?"

Sandra arranged for Rajiv to meet them in two hours at a nearby restaurant, and they walked into the tiny newspaper office. There wasn't much to see. Two of the three cluttered desks had no one seated at them, and the third showed only to top of a head behind a computer monitor. The head peeked around the monitor when the door closed behind them.

"Just dump it on that desk," the head said. An arm followed, and a finger pointed to the more cluttered of the two empty desks.

"Excuse me?" Sandra asked.

The head appeared again. Gray hair with bits of brown still making a valiant effort, dark rimmed glasses the only adornment. Sandra tried to guess the indeterminate gender and decided female, partly from the voice.

"You're not," she said, and changed her mind about completing the sentence when she saw Cocayne in her black leather pants, blue silk shirt, and long black hair dyed with a blue streak. "Of course not. What can I do for you?"

"We're looking for the entertainment desk," Sandra said.

"That'd be me," the woman said, gesturing at the other desks. "I'm all of them today. Most days. Bill is out drumming up more ad business, and Jill is down at the printers. What can the entertainment desk do for you?"

"Courtesy call," Sandra said. "I'm sure you're aware that *Full Auto* is playing at the Broken Pony tonight, and since the band usually sells out at most venues, we always invite the local media backstage before a show so they can meet the band, do interviews if they like, and see the show. Media gets in free, of course, and the first two drinks are on the band."

Sandra held a video recording pen in her hand, holding it steady on top of the monitor, panning it slowly across the desk as she spoke, not letting on that it was anything more than a pen. She held the CD in her other hand.

"We brought along a demo of the band's latest material," she said, holding the CD a little higher. "The band is doing a lot of unreleased material on the tour, so this is a recording we can't really let get out into the wild, but we like the local press to get a taste of what's to come on the next album."

96

Sandra walked around to the other side of the desk, aiming the pen camera at the monitor and the sticky notes attached to the frame around it. She turned the CD around in her hand. "Can we use your computer?" she asked, waving the CD and pointing it at the CD slot in the computer beside the desk.

"Um, sure," the entertainment desk editor said, overwhelmed by Sandra's unrelenting patter.

"I always ask," Sandra said, pushing the button to open the CD drive bay. "People are rightfully sensitive about who they let touch their computers." She inserted the disk and pushed the button to suck the CD into the computer.

"No problem," the woman said. A window popped up on the computer.

"Just hit enter," Sandra said. "It will start the first song. Do you have headphones? It will sound a lot better in headphones than in these little speakers," she said, pointing to the tiny boxes half hidden under stacks of paper. Sandra aimed the camera at one particular sticky note as the woman bent over a drawer to look for headphones.

"I don't think we have any headphones," she said, pawing through a drawer full of paper and office supplies.

"No big deal," Sandra said, as the sounds of *Full Auto* started to play over the tiny speakers. "You'll be getting to hear it live tonight. Nothing beats that."

Sandra put the pen back in her purse, and the three women listened in silence until the first song on the CD finished. She pushed the eject button before the next song could play.

"Have you got a piece of paper?" She asked the woman, as she reached for a pen from the jar of them under the monitor. "I'll write you a pass for tonight. We really have to be going, we're due at the radio station pretty soon. But we always like to give the print media the first shot, you know, they always have better writers."

The editor handed Sandra a note pad, and Sandra wrote *Backstage pass, print media, TJ Daniels*.

"Just show that at the door before the show starts at eight, and they'll let you in, give you the full tour. It's been great meeting you," she said, extending her hand.

97

"Um, thanks," the woman said, and Sandra turned and walked to the door, Cocayne in tow.

"Sold out?" Cocayne said as they walked down the sidewalk to the restaurant. "What happens when she shows up and the crowd looks like last night?"

"We can just say everyone's at the Jessie Carter concert. They're held over, and there's a lot of overlap in the fan base."

"There is?" Cocayne asked. "Who's Jessie Carter?"

"I have no idea," Sandra said. "But she's held over at the Pavilion. And she's cerebral."

They reached the restaurant. "Did you see what she was using as a password on her computer?" Sandra asked.

Cocayne gave her a puzzled look.

"I assume it was hers, there were three user names and three passwords on the note stuck to her monitor. Bill, Jill, and Janet. Did she seem like a cat person to you? Her password was K1ttyCat. With a 1 for the i, and capital K capital C. The software goes to such lengths to make them choose passwords with numbers and capital letters, and then they write it on a note and stick it on the computer. As if a password cracker couldn't have found that one anyway."

"A password cracker?"

"A program for cracking passwords. Wouldn't have worked in this case, since it would have taken forever. My next step would have been to install a key logger and accidentally trip over her power strip, but she made it too easy."

"You're planning on breaking into her computer?"

"I'm not breaking in. I asked politely. I have her on video giving me permission. Twice. Breaking into someone's computer is a federal offense these days. Always get permission, and if you can't get it in writing, and signed, get a video."

"Why do you need to get into her computer?"

"Did you see her face when she listened to the music? If she shows up, it will be for the free drinks. Besides, she's not going to write anything up that will get to people before tonight. No, what we want is her mailing list."

"What for?"

"It's a list of email addresses of lots of local people. Potential fans of *Full Auto*. They are all going to get an email right after lunch."

Right after lunch, Rajiv arrived to take them back to the Broken Pony. Once back in the bus, Sandra got to work.

She looked up Jessie Carter.

"Oh, this is good," she said to Cocayne. "Check out the outfit."

Cocayne looked at the photo of the singer. "Yeah?"

"We're going to have a Jessie Carter look-alike contest," Sandra said. "Blonde wig, beads, puffy shirt, that's an outfit someone can come up with in half an hour for Halloween."

She started typing, and Cocayne looked over her shoulder.

"We're Jessie Carter's favorite indy band?"

"Yup. She loves you guys. She's coming over tonight, so the newspaper is going to have a Jessie Carter look-alike contest here at the Broken Pony."

"She's really coming?"

"I doubt it. She'll be singing at the Pavilion. But you never know. I'll bet she's spotted by a bunch of people here tonight."

Sandra read over her handiwork, and logged into the newspaper's online newsletter account, and posted the review.

"Can we get in trouble for this?" Cocayne asked.

"If someone finds out what we did, sure," Sandra said. "But not jail-time kind of trouble. Just oops-I'm-sorry kind of trouble. I've been there a lot."

"I disavow any knowledge of this," Cocayne said, narrowing her eyes at Sandra in mock glare.

"Of course. And we'll fire that publicist right away, as soon as we can find him. We certainly won't be paying his bill."

Chapter 12: Would college have taught me where to hide the bodies?

Jack's feet were beginning to hurt.

He'd been standing at the reception counter at the hotel for over forty minutes, pretending to fill out an employment form left-handed. Several people had come and gone in that time, but no one had asked for Delia Santiago. But he had deliberately gotten here well before nine o'clock. The suspect would probably come by before ten, to get to Millbarque first. The next most probable time was after Jack had come and gone.

There was one Sacramento detective on a couch, pretending to read a newspaper. Another was in the car outside, watching one of Jeff Worthington's video screens. Gonzales was in the bar, out of sight, watching the other video screen. Gonzales had placed one camera behind the desk, facing the doorway. This provided a view of anyone walking in, but unfortunately the light was coming from behind, and all the people were silhouettes.

The other camera was looking down the long counter, and would get profile shots. Jack was at the far end, so as not to block the view.

A Sacramento SWAT vehicle was on alert, but not on the road, ready to come in as backup if things hit the fan.

Jack held the grip of his gun in his right hand, inside the pocket of his coat. He shifted his stance, trying to keep circulation in his toes.

Out of the corner of his eye, he saw a man approaching the counter. He was walking slowly and trying to survey the room without appearing to stare. *That coat could hide a nine-mil.* No one had walked in off the hot street in a coat except for Jack and the cop with the newspaper. Jack tensed.

The security man working the front desk shot a glance at Jack then back at the man. *Stay cool.*

The man cleared his throat. "I'm here to see one of your guests," he said. "The name is Delia Santiago."

The clerk almost squeaked. "Yes, yes, she's ex-expecting you," he said, too loudly, and he cleared his throat. Jack heard the rustle of a newspaper on the couch. His mouth was dry.

100

He kept his voice low. "Place both hands on the counter, and step back slowly." He moved so that the pocket of his coat pointed towards the man.

"I don't think so," the man said calmly. He turned just a little towards Jack, and Jack could see directly into the barrel of the gun in the man's left hand. The gun was not pointed at his chest, but at his head. A hard shot to make from waist high, but Jack could see that the aim was perfect. Someone was expecting him to be wearing a bullet-proof vest.

"Take off the coat slowly, and put it on the floor," the man said. Jack did not move. *If I shot him right now, would he get a round off?*

"I'm not alone," Jack said. "If you shoot me, you won't be walking out of here."

"You think I brought a fart to a shit fight?" the man said. "I have people all over this place."

"I'd do as he says," said the Sacramento detective. He had the newspaper folded over his right hand, which was pointing at the suspect.

"Freeze, both of you!" came a shout from the right. A man was standing in the breezeway, legs apart, both hands holding a gun at arm's length. He was aiming at the other detective.

"We seem to be at an impasse," the suspect said, his aim never wavering. He had not even looked at the other detective. His eyes had been locked on Jack's the whole time. "I'll ask you again. Place your jacket on the floor, slowly, and let me see your hands."

"Not going to happen," Jack said.

The big glass door behind the suspect eased open, and the second Sacramento detective eased in, his gun at eye level, aimed at the suspect's accomplice. "Put it down," he said to the man with the double-handed grip. The man shifted his wide stance but did not lower his weapon.

"Molino's not worth it," the suspect said to Jack. "Give it up, and you might live through this."

Jack tried not to move, not to give anyone a reason to start shooting. "Who is Molino?" he asked.

"Who is Delia Santiago?" the suspect asked.

"I actually haven't a clue," Jack said.

"What does she have for Molino?"

"Nothing. Millbarque isn't even here. That was just to get *you* to show up," Jack said.

"Who's Millbarque?"

Jack paused. "I am detective Jack Morgan, San Jose Police. The two other men pointing guns at you are Sacramento PD. SWAT is about to come crashing through the doors. Who the hell are you?"

Neither man moved a muscle.

"Sam Tyler, DEA."

"You got ID?" Jack asked.

The suspect called out to his accomplice. "Anderson, show them your ID." The gun was still aimed directly into Jack's face.

The accomplice shifted his stance and held his gun in his right hand as he reached into his pocket for his identification. He held it up. The second Sacramento detective walked slowly up to him, still aiming the gun, and inspected the credentials.

"He's DEA," he said.

Jack slowly lifted his left hand away from his body. "I'm going to remove my hand from my coat pocket," he said. He released his grip from the gun and eased his hand out. It was damp, and cramped. He held both hands out towards the first DEA agent. "Your turn," he said.

The agent placed his gun on the counter and showed his hands. The other DEA agent lowered his gun, and the two Sacramento detectives put theirs away and walked up to the counter. Gonzales came around from the bar.

"What the mother duck is going on here?" he said, joining the others. The security man behind the counter looked like he was going to be sick.

"We got played," Jack said. "He's not going to show up."

"Who isn't?" Tyler asked.

"We don't have a name. We're working a homicide. We set the suspect up to meet a Delia Santiago here."

Tyler grimaced. "We're working a Michoacán group led by Carlos Molino," he said. "Molino was supposed to meet Delia

Santiago here. She was supposed to have a ledger for him, a blackmail thing."

Jack looked at the other man. "When did you learn about that?"

"Late last night," Tyler said.

"You were set up," Jack said. "Our guy likes to put bugs in police stations. And key loggers on police computers. Sounds like he knew you were after Molino."

"We're going to want everything you have on your guy," Tyler said.

"Not a problem," Jack said. "We're already reporting everything to the marshals."

"There's a lot of that going around," Tyler said.

Jack walked over to one of the couches and sat down. He rubbed his legs. The others joined him.

"This is going to be a fun report to write up," Tyler said.

"At least I got comp'ed a room," Gonzales said. "You should check out the cookies they leave on the pillows."

The big doors burst open and several men in black flak jackets ran into the room.

"Everybody freeze!" the SWAT team leader shouted. Jack could not hold back a snort of laughter, and soon the whole group was laughing so hard tears were streaming down their faces. The SWAT team seemed completely unprepared for this reaction.

§

Gonzales drove, and Jack rode shotgun, his computer open, on his lap, trying to write up the events of the morning without causing himself any more humiliation or trouble than he knew he was in for. Lucky for him, it was a long drive.

"When you and your ex were dating, how did she react when you told her someone had been pointing a gun at you?" Gonzales asked.

"What makes you ask that?" Jack said.

"My girlfriend," Gonzales said. "I don't think she likes the idea of dating a cop. She worries."

"Liz pretty much handled everything the same way," Jack said. "She'd find a bottle to keep her company."

Gonzales chewed on that for a while.

"I'm not sure that helps me much," he said after a couple of miles.

"It never seemed to help her much either," Jack said.

"Is that why you two split up?"

"Hell no," Jack said. "I finally got her into rehab. Once she was sober for a few months, she figured out she really didn't like me much when she was sober."

Gonzales was quiet for another mile. "We've been partners for two years now. I've never heard you mention anyone but your ex."

"That's because there hasn't been anyone," Jack said.

"What's it been, four years almost? She must have been one piece of work."

It was Jack's turn to let the miles go by in silence. "She was one hell of a lawyer, even hung over," he finally said. "Sharp as hell. Real quick, too."

"Sounds like you still miss her," Gonzales offered quietly.

"I'm over it," Jack said. "But, yeah, I miss her. Just not when we run into each other in court. Then it's just uncomfortable."

Another few miles went by.

"So, what should I tell Vicky?" Gonzales asked.

Jack considered this. "The truth is usually best," he said. "Anything else gets complicated. If she can't handle it, it's probably best to find out early."

"Maybe I just won't tell her anything," Gonzales said.

Jack looked at his partner for a while. Gonzales finally took his eyes from the road and looked back.

"Yeah, shit," he said. "That probably won't work either."

Jack typed some more of his report into the computer. "Is this the girl your sister set you up with?"

"Yeah," Gonzales said.

"She probably knows all about you already."

"My sister probably made a whole bunch of shit up," Gonzales said. "Just to fuck with me."

"Like your time in prison?" Jack asked. "Or the serial killing spree? Or that you majored in nuclear forestry at MIT?"

"Maybe not that last part," Gonzales said.

"Too bad," Jack said. "That one was my favorite."

"I don't know," Gonzales said. "Would college have taught me where to hide the bodies?"

"I'm pretty sure that's covered in law school," Jack said.

"Yale then," Gonzales said. "Or maybe Harvard."

"Yeah, I'm betting she knows all about you already."

"Probably why she worries," Gonzales said, nodding.

"This part of my report, where you saved the day by using karate on the two guys with guns?"

"Probably shouldn't show her that," Gonzales said.

"I'll just make something up, then," Jack said. "Say you didn't come out until all the guns were put away."

"Hey!" Gonzales said. "That was the plan! I stay back and call SWAT if something goes wrong."

Jack laughed. "That was the plan. If I couldn't rely on you not doing something stupid, we wouldn't be partners."

"Damn straight," Gonzales said. There was quiet for another two miles. "Really?" he said, turning to look at Jack.

"We can't both be doing stupid things all the time," Jack said.

"Well, there *is* that," Gonzales said, nodding again.

§

Back at the Broken Pony, Cocayne went inside to resume practice, and Sandra took her computer back under the shade tree. It was too hot in the bus and too noisy inside with the band. She needed to find out what had happened in Sacramento.

Jack was online. She brought up the video window and waited for his face to appear. When it did, he didn't say anything at first, just studied what he saw on his screen.

"Hi there," Sandra said. "Something wrong?"

"No," Jack said. "Just looking at the shadows behind you. Trying to see what time zone you're in. I'm not believing Beijing."

"Oaxaca," she said. "Too bad you can't see the view of the ocean from here."

"That's funny," Jack said. "We didn't get any alerts from the border crossings. I'll have to look up the weather report."

"He didn't show, did he," Sandra said. It would have been the first thing out of Jack's mouth.

"He played us," Jack said. "Sent a couple DEA agents there to ask for your friend. Things got a little tense before we both caught on."

"How tense?" Sandra asked.

"Guns drawn, Mexican standoff. Two of them, four of us, good thing we got it all straightened out before SWAT busted in, that could have been messy."

"Jack!" Sandra said, alarmed. "Shit, I should have never said, I mean, I thought I was helping. You could have been killed."

"Same as if the guy had shown up," Jack said. "We knew he was dangerous. That's why I had my gun out. Turned out the other guy did, too."

"Shit. He knew it was a trick, that part I can see. But how did he get someone to show up and pull a gun on you?"

"My new friends at the DEA are looking into that. They were working a case and got a tip late last night that their guy was showing up at the Hilton asking for Delia Santiago. Who the hell is Delia Santiago, anyway?"

"My high school math teacher. She retired after that semester."

"You seem to have quite an effect on people," Jack said.

"Look at you being funny," Sandra said. "You should get this kind of adrenaline more often. You're almost human."

Jack studied her face for a while.

"The funeral's tomorrow," he said.

"Shit," Sandra said.

"Don't think of showing up," Jack said. "We're hoping he'll be there, looking for you, or for clues about where you are."

"Poor Scott. He has a sister, I know that. If his parents are still around, they'd have to be ninety or something."

Jack was silent for half a minute. "Will there be anyone there who knows what you look like?" he asked.

"Don't even try it. What if he's half a mile away with a sniper rifle? She'd be dead, and you'd be no better off."

"Just a thought," Jack said.

"You'll be setting up video, right?"

"Probably a good idea. We usually have guys with long lenses in cars with tinted windows," Jack said.

"This guy is smart. He'll see those, and you'll never get a shot that's any good. Use the little guys that Jeff gave you. Stick them on something with a good view and record the whole thing from a couple different angles. If you send me the video, I can eliminate all the good guys and do a face search for the others."

"I can't send it to you. It's evidence," Jack said.

"It isn't evidence until it's logged as evidence," Sandra said. "I know how you guys do things. Email it to me first thing, then you can write it up later."

"Why would I do that?" Jack asked.

"Because you guys can't use the Homeland Security facial recognition database without a lot of paperwork, and maybe a warrant."

"And you can?" Jack asked.

"I don't need warrants," Sandra said. "And some people owe me favors, and some others want favors from me. I can be useful, Jack. Let me have something to work with."

"I'll think it over," Jack said. "I'm not making any promises."

"Then I won't ask for any," she said. "You've already had a big enough day today." She looked at the time showing at the bottom of her screen. "I should go," she said. "You be really careful, OK?"

He studied her face again. "We'll get this guy," he said.

"Damn right we will," she said and winked, then closed the window.

She felt like she was slipping into deep water and had nothing to hang onto.

She took one last deep breath and wished she had learned how to swim.

Wasting no more time, she looked up Jeff Worthington and found he was online as well. She brought up the video window again and waited.

"Hi there," Jeff said, looking pleased with himself.

"Yes, I need another favor," Sandra said.

§

Jack had been home for two hours, working on his report, when the computer announced that Sandra Millbarque wanted to start a video chat. He clicked on the OK button, and her face showed up on the screen. She was leaning against a tree, and he could see shadows on the ground behind her of buildings and another tree. She seemed to be sitting on grass, from the looks of the scene behind her.

"Hi there," she said. "Something wrong?"

He filled her in on the day's activities and told her about the funeral the next day. She seemed concerned more for Jack and Tremain's family than for her own predicament. Was she really that cool, or did she just have a good poker face? Again, he got the impression that she knew more than she was telling, or that she was two steps ahead of everyone else in this game.

After her face had disappeared from his screen, he called Gonzales on the phone.

"You still have those video gadgets, right?" he asked.

"Out in the car," Gonzales said.

"Copy the video off of them and erase them, so we have plenty of room. And charge them up. We're going to want them at the funeral tomorrow."

"You talked to the chick, didn't you."

"Yes, I did," Jack said.

"She's not showing up, or you wouldn't be asking about the cameras."

"She said the guy was probably sitting somewhere with a sniper rifle waiting for someone who looked like her to show her face there."

"The strangle wire guy has a sniper rifle?" Gonzales asked.

"He's careful never to use the same M.O. twice," Jack said. "But he hasn't used a rifle yet, as far as we know."

"You don't buy the guy liking close up work, getting off on it," Gonzales said.

"The other jobs weren't close," Jack said. "I think he needed something from Tremain, risked showing his face in order to get it."

109

"Think he got what he needed?"

"I don't even know what he was after," Jack said. "It's just a feeling. And I think the blood splatter was done after he put Tremain's body in the office on the chair. Explains why no footprints in the blood. He wants us to think it happened in the office."

"Where did it really happen?"

"Somewhere that would tie the killing to the killer. Like his car, or something," Jack said.

"Does that help us?"

"Have Jimmy check all the rental car agencies for muscle cars rented during that timeframe. Have him check them for blood or bleach."

"He likes muscle cars. That was on the disk," Gonzales said.

"I think everything we need is on that disk," Jack said. "We just have to figure out what to do with all that information."

Chapter 13: The trouble with cashmere is it's so hard to get the blood out.

The first car arrived a little after six o'clock. Sandra looked up from her computer when she heard the noise of their radio blaring through the open windows of the car. The bass was turned way up, and the car seemed to thump with every beat as if it was going to slowly bounce back into the street.

A few minutes later they were joined by another car, and the competing sound systems made it impossible to think, let alone use the computer anymore. Sandra stood up and walked to the back door of the Broken Pony. Another car arrived as she opened the door.

The band was on stage, no longer practicing, but adjusting the sound on the monitors.

"The bus is locked up, right?" Sandra called up to Cocayne.

"I think so, why?"

"We have company outside. Three cars, maybe a dozen people, two or three of them still sober," Sandra said.

Maria at the bar looked up. "We don't open until eight o'clock," she said. "Why do they come so early?"

"Maybe to beat the crowds," Sandra said. Everyone laughed.

Someone was banging on the door, and Maria went to see who it was. A shaft of late afternoon sunlight momentarily lit up the normally dim interior. The band members blinked at the sudden brightness, but Sandra could see several people through the doorway, one of them in a long blonde wig, puffy white blouse, and Mardi Gras beads. Only the beard spoiled the effect.

"We don't open until eight o'clock," Maria repeated to the crowd, pointing to the sign on the door. There were some sounds of complaint, but mostly just sounds of people milling about. The door closed, and Sandra waited for her eyes to readjust to the dark club.

"They're lining up," Maria said. "They're not going away."

"You make that sound like a bad thing," Sandra said.

"We never have a line," Maria said.

"I think we found out why, this morning," Sandra said, looking up at Cocayne on the stage.

111

Cocayne jumped down. "There's really a line of people out there?" she asked. She walked to the back door and went outside. She was back inside in less than a minute.

"Shit, there's like a dozen cars out there," she said. She had barely locked the back door when they heard someone banging on it.

"I better call Mr. Jerry," Maria said. "We're going to need more help tonight."

"Maybe a bouncer or two," Cocayne said, as more banging came from the back door.

By a quarter to seven, the parking lot was full, and people were starting to park on the street, and at the Laundromat next door. Jerry Cortero, the owner of the Broken Pony, had to phone Maria to be let in, since no one inside was answering any of the many times people were banging on the doors.

The first thing Jerry did was to call the police and ask for assistance. Then he went back outside to try to control the crowd and get them to line up in a more orderly fashion. The first police arrived in less than five minutes, and by seven o'clock there were several off-duty police on Jerry's payroll to assist in crowd control.

"Can you guys start a little early?" Jerry called up to Cocayne, on the stage again.

She gave a glance behind her at the rest of the band, and Pocket started the drum introduction to the first set. Charlie joined in on the bass, and the doors opened, and people started streaming into the club.

By eight o'clock, it was clear that the tables were only getting in the way, and Sandra, two policemen, and half a dozen volunteers from the crowd started moving them out the back door.

Jerry was still outside, taking money and stamping hands, to speed the flow of people into the club, when the police stopped him, because there was no more room inside. More people continued to arrive. The band took a break at nine o'clock, and came out to see the crowd.

"How about we put some amps and speakers in the parking lot, for all the rest of these people?" Cocayne asked. In the end, Jerry opened all the doors to the club, and Sandra helped set up speakers

112

just outside, putting gaffer's tape on the cables on the floor while trying to keep her fingers from getting trampled.

The band started back up, and people started dancing out in the parking lot and in the street where the police had blocked traffic. Sandra looked up at Cocayne on the stage, the microphone in her hand, her head back, singing as loudly as she could, taking in the crowd and the noise. It looked like this was her idea of heaven.

At two in the morning, the crowd showed no signs of thinning out. A second shift of off-duty policemen replaced the first, and the band started repeating some of the songs they had performed earlier in the evening. Pocket had removed his shirt but was still dripping with sweat. Cocayne looked exhausted but jubilant as they took another break. Sandra met her in the line to use the women's restroom.

"We're going to have to give our new publicist a cut of the take," Cocayne said to her, cupping her hands near Sandra's ear to be heard.

Sandra shook her head. "No way. I can take credit for some of the first ones to arrive, maybe, but I didn't make them stay, and I didn't make them call all their friends to come to the party. That's all you guys. All these people still here? That's all you."

Inside the packed restroom, a young woman stood stripped to her bra, washing a sweater in the sink. The wash water was bright red.

"Are you OK?" Cocayne asked.

"Yeah. Some jerk popped my boyfriend in the nose with his elbow, and I got blood all over me." She continued to rinse out the sweater.

Cocayne found a soap dispenser that still had some detergent and brought a handful over to help.

The girl held the sweater under the water again, and pink suds filled the basin. "That's the trouble with cashmere, it's so hard to get the blood out."

Cocayne laughed loudly. "I'm going to have to use that line in a song," she said.

The girl looked up at her. "Omigod! You're with the band!"

Cocayne patted her shoulder and escaped into a newly opened stall.

By the time Sandra got out of the next available stall, the woman was drying the sweater under an air drier. Cocayne was making her way out the door, anxious not to make the break take too long.

"That's going to shrink like crazy," Sandra said, washing her hands.

"Cool!" said the young woman. Sandra wondered how pink the sweater had been before the accident.

Back out in the club, Sandra heard a familiar stuttering drum rhythm and looked up at the stage. Cocayne was holding her microphone at her waist, pointing at the ground, and Link was playing the guitar, his mouth close to the mike on the stand.

"Got a five-legged dog," he sang. Cocayne was shaking her head sadly, but she raised the microphone to her lips and joined in the next line. "He don't walk too well."

Sandra looked out at the crowd. Some were still trying to dance, but no one seemed able to find the rhythm. Eventually most of the crowd just started swaying together. The noise of the crowd started to wane as people got caught up in the intricate patterns of the guitars and drums. She rocked back and forth with the crowd, listening to the harmonies Cocayne was adding to Link's melody.

When the song ended, the crowd broke into applause, and Cocayne stepped forward on the stage, speaking into the microphone.

"That's the show," she said. "We're *Full Auto*, and you can buy our CDs at the bar, or come by tomorrow, or you can get them on our web site."

Several people in the crowd started shouting for songs they had heard earlier, calling out pieces of chorus for songs whose titles they didn't know. Cocayne listened to them for a while, and then turned back to the band. Pocket started drumming, and the crowd broke into applause again at the encore.

It was almost four in the morning when the last of the crowd had gone, and all the tables had been brought back into the club.

Cocayne was leaning on Link for support, pantomiming how exhausted she was.

As the last light in the bus went out, and they were all in their bunks, Sandra heard Link ask, "We get a cut of the gate, right?"

"Yes, we do," Cocayne said.

"Shit," Pocket whispered. "We made *bank* tonight!"

§

No one got up early the next morning. It was almost noon when the smell of coffee brought Sandra out of her slumber. She lifted her head to see Cocayne pouring a cup. The others were still asleep, or faking it well. She pulled on some clothes under the blanket and slipped out of the bunk to join Cocayne. The two carried their coffee cups outside the bus so they could talk without waking the others.

The parking lot still needed quite a bit of cleanup. Cocayne surveyed the wreckage.

"That was kick-ass awesome," she said.

"It will be interesting to see what happens tonight," Sandra said. "The word is out. They'll tell their friends. It will probably be in this morning's newspaper."

"But we won't be advertising," Cocayne said. "No look-alike contest, no emails, no blog comments, no Google ads."

"You were taking notes."

"Damn right. I don't think I'm up to stealing mailing lists, though," Cocayne said.

"Probably for the best."

They walked into the Broken Pony. It looked like it was living up to its name. Jerry Cortero and four women were working, cleaning and repairing. Cortero looked up when they came in.

"Now I know what they mean when they say be careful what you wish for," he said. "You know how much it costs to rent crowd control from off-duty cops?"

"I'm sure I'll find out when we see our cut of the gate," Cocayne said, chuckling.

"No, I have to eat that," Cortero said. "Our agreement was for gross receipts, not net."

"So, you're in the hole for last night?" Cocayne asked.

"No, it was still a better night than we've had all year. Of course, I haven't finished paying for the cleanup, but we're looking pretty good. After the first night, I thought we were in for business as usual."

Sandra looked at Cocayne and quickly said, "Yeah, the band grows on people like that."

116

"But we don't have any idea what tonight will be like," Cocayne said.

"We'll be ready. If it turns out we don't need so much help, I can let them go early."

The two women refilled their coffee cups behind the bar and walked back out into the sunshine. Sandra picked up some litter and put it into the empty trashcan it had been sitting next to.

"I don't know about people," she said.

"Somebody else's problem," Cocayne said. "There's a song in that, somewhere."

"You're doing that all the time, aren't you? Thinking about the next song you're going to write."

"Pretty much," Cocayne said. "We ran out of material last night. Almost had to resort to covers. Did some really old crap we hadn't rehearsed in months, stuff we're not really proud of."

"How long does it take to write a song?"

"One of my favorites only took an afternoon. Others we keep working on for weeks. Tonight, though, I'm going to have Link and Charlie jam for a while in the middle of a few, stretch it out. Unless nobody shows up."

The windows on the bus started opening, and bunks were lowered to let the air flow through. The bus was still mostly in the shade, but later in the afternoon it would be unlivably hot.

"Looks like the guys are up. I'm going to the Y to take a shower."

Sandra went inside to get her computer. Today was Scott's funeral, and Jeff's live feed was probably already up. She took the computer to the relatively cool spot of shade on the grass and found Worthington's email with the link to the video feed.

As usual, Worthington was showing off. There were three video feeds. One was placed behind the guest book, so that it would record the names of the guests as they signed in, and their faces as they approached. The names were upside down, but Sandra could read some of them without turning her computer around. Another was in the van, watching all the cars that came into the parking lot. License plates and the faces of people as they left their cars would be visible. The third was moving, apparently on Worthington himself, as it focused on the face of the minister.

There were buttons below each feed, controlling the sound, and one extra one on the moving feed, that allowed her to speak to Worthington. She hesitated by that one. Best to wait until he was alone, in case others could hear. She got her headset out of her purse and plugged it into the computer, adjusting the boom microphone as she put on the headset. Now she could listen in privately and block the street noise.

While watching the people on the screen, she pulled up her email. The one from her sister could wait. She knew what it would say, and she wasn't prepared to deal with that right now. She read and discarded some others that did not need her attention. Then she saw the one from Balrog a few lines down and jumped immediately to read that one.

Got a ping in my watch file about you.

Marshals have you on a school bus with kids headed out of Sacramento.

No plates for the bus, kids have cocaine on board.

If this is one of your feints, it's working. If not, trouble is coming your way.

Sandra leaned back against the tree. She knew this would happen, but she didn't think it would be so soon. When you get comfortable, you get sloppy. The marshals knew about the bus. She should leave today, or tonight.

Worthington was still talking to the minister. She clicked on the button to listen in.

"...so, you'd not only have all your sermons available on video, but you'd have an indication of how well the audience was responding to every part. We can track eye movement, blink rates, correlated movements. It really is the latest thing in audience monitoring. You could then refine your message, fix the parts where they tune out, find out what gets them excited. What do you say?"

"It still sounds like spying on my parishioners," the minister said.

118

"The cameras don't see anything more than you see. They'd be mounted right behind you."

Worthington was scanning around the grounds as he spoke, and he saw something and stopped talking. The video was difficult to track when it was moving, but now that it had settled on a subject, Sandra could see Jack Morgan and Jaime Gonzales.

"Gentlemen," Worthington said, and the camera blurred quickly and settled on the minister again. "Excuse me, padre," he said, and there was a loud thump and then, "I should let you mingle." The video rushed once again to focus on the detectives.

Sandra clicked on the button that let her talk to Worthington. "I'm here," she said. The camera view dipped and then lifted, as the man nodded. *It must be mounted on his head.*

"I hear things got pretty hairy in Sacramento," he said. "I expect that video isn't going to go public until you're ready to publish your memoirs. Too bad, I was really hoping you'd get the guy. Scott was a good man. And that video would have been worth a nice chunk of change to the right news outlets."

"You hear that from Millbarque?" Morgan asked.

"We had a chat. She said to say hi."

"She working on her tan?"

Sandra almost laughed. "He's fishing," she said quickly.

"That sounds like you're fishing for something, detective," Worthington said. "Why don't you just ask? We're on the same team here."

"We tracked her down to a McDonald's in Oaxaca."

"He did not," Sandra said. "I fed him that."

"The one that got firebombed?" Worthington asked.

"What's that?"

"Had to be. There's only one McDonald's in Oaxaca, I'm pretty sure. There was that big stink when they wanted to put it in the main square, so they put it in that shopping center, and then someone threw a Molotov in there anyway, back in oh six. The wife and I went there in oh eight for a vacation. She likes history."

"So, you know the place," Morgan said.

"We didn't go to the McDonald's, if that's what you're asking. We prefer authentic local stuff when we travel. You can get a burger anywhere."

"Don't mention I was with you guys," Sandra said quickly.

"What did she call you about?" Morgan asked.

"She said you weren't going to give her any shots from today. Asked if I would shoot some video of everyone who shows up. Asked if I'd make sure some people knew the funeral was today."

"Which people would that be?"

"Shoot him the email I sent you," Sandra said.

"You want the list?" Worthington asked, pulling out a cell phone from his pocket. "I can forward her email to you. She had eleven people she wanted to know. She said she wasn't sure the sister would know to invite them, since she's from out of town." He played with the phone for a minute and found the email. "What's your address?"

"You already have his email address," Sandra said, but she heard Morgan repeat it.

"Anyone you know on the list?" Morgan asked.

"A couple," Worthington said. "Local reporter, and one of Scott's clients I've done business with. These guys are just the ones she didn't have email addresses for, so I assume she got the word out to more than just eleven."

"Why would she want a lot of people here?"

"So that the family would know he had friends here," he said. "Everybody liked Scott. A lot of people would have been disappointed if they missed a chance to say goodbye. I would have been."

"Me too," Sandra said.

"So," Morgan said, "Where did you set up your cameras?"

"Don't give him the guest book camera," Sandra said. "Just the one you're wearing."

"Check this out," she heard Worthington say. "It stores five hours of video. Anything I point my head at. Wide-angle view, audio's not the best, but hey, it's only two hundred bucks. And it actually works as a hands-free earpiece for the phone. And check this out," he said, and there was considerable blurring as the camera faced the ground, and then showed Worthington's hands holding a cell phone. Then there was a loud rustling and a lot of blurry video, and then the picture settled on the chapel. "Now I have eyes in the back of my head," she heard Worthington say.

"Looks like you're all set," Morgan said. "We should get moving. Work to do."

Sandra watched as the two detectives walked away.

"You are such a show-off," she said to Worthington.

"And I get to play with all the best toys," he said.

The camera watched the two detectives, each with a cell phone to his ear.

"That looks a little obvious," Sandra said.

"They work with what they have," Worthington replied. "At least they turned off the flash. Most people see a cell phone to someone's ear, not a camera facing them."

"You're collecting cell phone signal timing, right?" Sandra asked.

"Of course."

"I can get a list of the calls from that area during the service," Sandra said. "If we can match the timing to a pre-paid cell number, we'll know our guy was there, and we'll have his number."

"I thought you already had his numbers," Worthington said.

"They all went quiet when the marshals got the disk," Sandra said. "Either his ears in the station tipped him off, or he has ears at the marshals' as well."

"You're assuming he has everything on the disk," Worthington said.

"And he has my honeypots, so he won't make that mistake again. But he was over at Sharon's a couple nights ago. She sent me an email about it. Unfortunately, she didn't get a good look at him. As soon as you see her, go tell her I'm OK and that I got her message. She doesn't have a secure email setup, so I didn't reply to it."

"She should be arriving pretty soon," Worthington said. "The service is about ready."

"Tell her I said it's OK to trust Jack Morgan," Sandra said. "Scott had her afraid to talk to the police."

"Good advice, considering they were bugged."

"You can tell her that. She might feel better knowing we're making progress. And that five of Scott's best muscle guys are hanging around the service, just in case."

"I wondered who those guys were."

"And now Jack Morgan knows I invited them, so he won't assume they're on the wrong side. I think more than one of them has some embarrassing history with the local law."

"I see Sharon coming in now," Worthington said. Sandra could see her on the screen.

"Jeff, I'm going to have to go. The marshals have tracked down how I left Sacramento, and they'll find this place by tomorrow or the next day. I may be out of reach for a day or two, while I relocate."

"You don't want to talk to Sharon," he said.

"I can't handle that right now. We'd both end up in tears, and it'd be a mess. Say hi for me."

"I'll do that."

"Put the video up on House of Pain. The passphrase is 'He was so polite over tea that she almost regretted the arsenic.' Capital H, period at the end. That way Balrog can get to it."

"You have a morbid sense of humor," Worthington said.

"Makes them easier to remember. Gotta go." Sandra disconnected and took off the headphones. She leaned her head back against the tree and let the tears come.

§

Cocayne was upset. "You're leaving? Today? Just like that?"

"They found out I left Sacramento with you guys. By tomorrow they'll figure out we're here. Either federal marshals will pick me up, or someone much worse. And if I'm not there when they get here, you won't be harboring a fugitive."

"That just sucks," Pocket said. "What if you hide out until they're gone, and then come back?"

"Or meet us in Tucson at the next gig," Link offered.

"I need to lead them away from you," Sandra said. "Trust me, you really want no part of this. I should never have put you guys in this situation. It was really selfish of me."

They argued for a while, but everyone knew she had to leave. The conversation turned to how to stay in touch, and what was going to happen next.

"The only way this is going to end is when the guy gets caught," Sandra said. "I've baited him with lies, but he saw through them. The only way this can work is to actually make him move, and for that I need to give him something he knows is real. Me."

"You're going to let him kill you?" Pocket was confused.

"No, but I have to let him find me. Before the marshals or the police do. Then I have to make sure he doesn't catch me."

"Why don't you just leave the country or something?" Link asked.

"I'm pretty sure I'm on the 'Don't fly' list already. And I'd be easier to find in Mexico than here, where I can blend in and disappear. And Canada would be no better. He could still follow me, and then I wouldn't have the marshals or the police when I need them."

"Then you're the bait. What's the plan?" Cocayne was still upset.

"I need to find out who he is. Once I know that, I can tell the marshals and the police, and they take it from there. I need to draw him out. Make him move, make him use his phone, or his credit cards, get a picture of his face, something like that. If I move around, and he follows me, all of that gets a lot easier. It's called stochastic sifting, and it's something I do all the time in my job."

123

"Just move around?"

"No. The way people get caught most frequently is that they have to be somewhere specific for some reason. He knows about my mom. He'll be watching to see if I visit. I'm going to visit my mother."

Cocayne shook her head. "He's waiting for you to see your mother. And you're going to walk right into whatever trap he has waiting for you, and hope he gives himself away before he gets you."

"I'll be pushing the odds a little more in my favor," Sandra said.

"Six chambers, one bullet," Cocayne said.

"Hopefully a little better than that."

Chapter 14: He might have been faithful if he knew she owned a gun.

Gonzales was already in the chapel courtyard when Jack arrived. The ceremony would be nearby, under a large tree, and finding places from which to view all possible onlookers was going to be difficult. A broad lawn, ending in a wrought-iron fence that ran alongside a busy street, meant that any of the passing cars would have a view of the proceedings, however brief. Opposite the lawn was a parking lot, which also would present problems.

"Too bad we only have two cameras," Jack said as he caught up with Gonzales.

"Yeah," Gonzales replied. "Looks like we'll have to use the cell phone trick after all."

Jack looked towards the chapel. "Upstairs window?" he asked.

"Unless we can get up on the roof," Gonzales said. "They have magnets. We could stick one on the vent pipe, if there's an easy way to get on the roof without attracting a lot of attention."

Jack looked around. "If we have one up there," he said, pointing at the chapel, "We'll want the other one to pick up the view from that direction." He pointed opposite the chapel. Nothing in particular stood out as a good spot, but there was the wrought-iron fence not too far from the ideal location. They walked in that direction.

"You know he's not going to show," Gonzales said.

"We have to try," Jack said. "We might get lucky. He might send someone. He might pull some trick like at the Hilton, and tip his hand in some way."

Jack stuck the camera to the fence and tested the view on the handheld receiver. They walked back to the chapel to install the other camera.

"Oh shit," Gonzales said. "Look who showed up."

Jack turned off the video receiver and put it into a pocket. He handed the other camera to Gonzales.

"See if you can get this up there without these clowns seeing you," he said. "I'd rather they didn't know about the videos."

"No problem. I didn't want to talk to them anyway." Gonzales headed off to the right to avoid the two marshals, and Jack continued walking towards them.

125

"So," the fat marshal said as the gap between them narrowed. "I hear we were both in the same neighborhood yesterday."

Jack stopped. "You were in Sacramento?" he asked.

"Closing in on the suspect you couldn't find," the fat man said. "The Millbarque woman. Found the guy who drove her car home for her. Name of Rafael Martinez. Said she's on a school bus with some kids."

"You've got her as a suspect, not a person of interest?" Jack asked.

"Someone in WITSEC is leaking information to her, and she's selling it. That's a federal crime."

"One of your people is sending her information?" Jack asked.

"Has to be. She sold Johnson to the Melone gang."

"Johnson's dead," Jack said. "There's no point anymore in pretending Melone was involved."

"What do you know about that?" the fat man said.

Bingo. Thanks for confirming that hunch. Jack stepped a little closer to the shorter man.

"This partnership seems to be suffering from a one-way communication problem. And I'm not the idiot you seem to think I am. Let's have a chat sometime when you have something interesting to say." Jack stepped around the fat man and headed towards the chapel. Gonzales had just closed the upstairs window, and it was no longer necessary to keep the two men facing away from it.

The thin man spoke, the first time Jack had ever heard his voice. "Are you expecting Millbarque to show?"

Jack stopped and turned towards him. The man was slim waisted, but only thin in comparison to his fat shadow. He had broad shoulders and carried himself like an athlete.

"Someone told me she was in Oaxaca," Jack said.

"You're looking for a second killer," the slim man said.

"She didn't kill Tremain," Jack said. "I'm looking for someone wearing a Cartier watch, driving a muscle car, wears lambskin gloves, and packs a nine-mil. You see him around, give me a call, OK?"

126

"We'll do that," the marshal said, touching his finger to his forehead in a mock salute.

As the walked in their separate directions, Jack could hear the fat man ask, "Who's she in hock to?"

Jack met up with Gonzales as he was coming out of the chapel, watching the video receiver in his hand as he walked.

"How's the view?" Jack asked.

"Not great. We'll still need the cell phone trick. But the cameras should help. We'll get angles we can't get from the ground."

Workers were setting up folding chairs on the lawn. The two detectives walked over to the parking lot and sat on a stone bench to await the arrival of the mourners. Jack noticed a familiar van parked in the lot.

"Did you see Worthington anywhere?" he asked Gonzales.

"The spy gadget guy?" he followed Jack's pointing finger to see the van. "No, think he's just here to pay respects?"

"He did do business with the deceased," Jack said. "But we should keep an eye on him."

"What, does he look like a Scotch drinker to you?" Gonzales asked.

"He knows all the right people," Jack said. "He knows how to avoid getting caught by Millbarque. He might even have ears in the DEA."

"Tremain would have trusted him. Easy to get him into a car," Gonzales said.

"Or a van." Jack looked at the van again. "Did you smell any bleach the last time we were close?"

"He'd know to use oxygen bleach, that it works better than chlorine to get rid of DNA. And you can't smell it."

Jack took out his notebook. "It would be interesting to find out if he flies coach," he said.

"And he did seem really happy to be helping out Millbarque," Gonzales said. "For free, even."

"If we were to mention she was in Oaxaca," Jack said, "I wonder if he'd suddenly be out of town."

"Not specific enough," Gonzales said. "And if it was, he'd just phone first, and check it out."

127

"Which he might do even if he wasn't our guy," Jack said.

"It has to be somewhere without a phone, but easy to find on foot."

"How about she's using a McDonald's for Internet access?" Jack asked.

"Worth a try. Do they have a McDonald's there?"

Jack shrugged. A blue sedan pulled into the parking lot. A tan station wagon pulled in after it.

"Looks like people are starting to arrive," Jack said. "We should probably mingle."

The two men stood up, and walked back to the chapel courtyard. Jeff Worthington was standing in front of the array of folding chairs, talking to the minister. The minister was dressed in a suit and tie, while Worthington was more appropriately dressed for the weather, in short sleeves and slacks.

"Does that look like a ten thousand dollar watch to you?" Jack asked Gonzales.

"Maybe if they sell 'em by the pound," he said.

On either side of a small podium there were tables draped in dark blue, with arrays of flowers nearly covering them. There was no casket. This was to be a ceremony only. Jack wondered if Tremain had willed his body to a medical school. That was not one of the questions he was going to ask today.

"Gentlemen," Worthington said as he caught sight of the two detectives. "Excuse me, padre," he said to the minister, tapping the large Bluetooth earpiece over his right ear. "I should let you mingle."

He walked over to Jack and Gonzales. "I hear things got pretty hairy in Sacramento," he said. "I expect that video isn't going to go public until you're ready to publish your memoirs. Too bad, I was really hoping you'd get the guy. Scott was a good man. And that video would have been worth a nice chunk of change to the right news outlets."

"You hear that from Millbarque?" Jack asked.

"We had a chat. She said to say hi."

"She working on her tan?" Jack asked.

Worthington looked at him carefully. "That sounds like you're fishing for something, detective," he said. "Why don't you just ask? We're on the same team here."

"We tracked her down to a McDonald's in Oaxaca," Jack said. He watched Worthington's face carefully. The man seemed to be thinking too much about what he was going to say next.

"The one that got firebombed?" Worthington asked.

"What's that?"

"Had to be. There's only one McDonald's in Oaxaca, I'm pretty sure. There was that big stink when they wanted to put it in the main square, so they put it in that shopping center, and then someone threw a Molotov in there anyway, back in oh six. The wife and I went there in oh eight for a vacation. She likes history."

"You know the place," Jack said.

"We didn't go to the McDonald's, if that's what you're asking. We prefer authentic local stuff when we travel. You can get a burger anywhere."

Jack waited for any sign that Worthington was interested in Millbarque's location, but he couldn't read anything into the man's chattiness. "What did she call you about?" he asked.

"She said you weren't going to give her any shots from today. Asked if I would shoot some video of everyone who shows up. Asked if I'd make sure some people knew the funeral was today."

"Which people would that be?" Jack asked. Again, Worthington seemed to think too long.

"You want the list?" Worthington asked, pulling out a cell phone from his pocket. "I can forward her email to you. She had eleven people she wanted to know. She said she wasn't sure the sister would know to invite them, since she's from out of town." He played with the phone for a minute and found the email. "What's your address?"

Jack gave him his office email address, and Worthington sent the list.

"Anyone you know on the list?" he asked.

"A couple," Worthington said. "Local reporter, and one of Scott's clients I've done business with. These guys are just the ones she didn't have email addresses for, so I assume she got the word out to more than just eleven."

"Why would she want a lot of people here?" Jack asked.

Worthington seemed surprised at the question. "So that the family would know he had friends here," he said. "Everybody liked Scott. A lot of people would have been disappointed if they missed a chance to say goodbye. I would have been."

She probably also wanted a lot of eyes and ears, boots on the ground.

People were beginning to arrive and mill around. "So," Jack said, "Where did you set up your cameras?"

Worthington smiled. "Check this out," he said, pointing to the Bluetooth earpiece over his ear. "It stores five hours of video. Anything I point my head at. Wide-angle view, audio's not the best, but hey, it's only two hundred bucks. And it actually works as a hands-free earpiece for the phone. And check this out," he said, pulling the phone out of his pocket again. He touched some controls on the screen, and after a few seconds Jack could see his face on the display. Worthington took the device off of his right ear and put it on his left, with the boom facing backwards. "Now I have eyes in the back of my head."

"Looks like you're all set," Jack said. "We should get moving," he said to Gonzales. "Work to do," he said to Worthington.

They walked behind the podium and the flowers, where they could see many of the faces of the people in the courtyard. The staff was bringing out more folding chairs, as the crowd was getting larger than had been expected.

Gonzales had his cell phone to his ear, as if he were talking to someone. But Jack could see his finger repeatedly pressing the shutter release button to photograph the crowd. Jack took his own phone out and set it to record video. He held it to his ear and slowly turned, to sweep through as many people as he could, but without motion blur.

The two detectives walked around the crowd, getting as many faces as possible, always staying conspicuously busy on their cell phones. Gonzales occasionally stooped to pick something out of the grass when one visitor or another seemed to never lift their head enough.

Jack stopped when he saw the woman come out of the chapel, accompanied by four men and two small children. He figured she must be Tremain's sister. There were no other children in the crowd. He had spoken to her on the phone, after the captain had broken the news about her brother's death. He was not looking forward to speaking with her again but knew that was part of the job. He aimed the cell phone camera in their direction, looking at the screen as if reading some message there.

Worthington joined the small group and offered his hand to the woman, and they spoke for a while. Jack saw him look up, and gesture that he should join the group. *Shit.* Jack walked over.

"Sharon, I'd like you to meet Jack Morgan. He's the detective on the case."

She held out her hand. "We've spoken on the phone," she said.

"Tell Jack about the prowler," Worthington said.

"It's probably nothing at all," she said tentatively. "Some guy walking around the house. He didn't break in or anything. But he was inside the fence."

"When was this?" Jack asked.

"Two nights ago," she said. "Like I said, it's probably nothing. But it was three in the morning. The neighbor's dog woke us up, barking. I thought it was another raccoon, but I got up and looked out the window, and he was there."

"Can you describe him?"

"Well, it was pretty dark. He was tall though. He could see over the fence. I saw him looking at the dog. He didn't need to stand on his toes, he could just see over."

"So, maybe six two, or six three?" Jack asked.

"I really can't say. It's a normal-size fence."

"Was there anything else about him you can describe?"

"He was wearing dark clothes. He had short hair, maybe brown, or maybe light brown."

"Beard, mustache, balding?" Jack asked.

"No, just normal."

"Heavy set, thin, what kind of clothes?"

131

"Normal. Long sleeves, I think, or maybe a windbreaker. Oh, and he was carrying a purse!"

"A purse," Jack said. "What kind of a purse?"

"Black, kind of big. Heavy, I think, because of the way he carried it."

"If you saw him here in the crowd, do you think you would recognize him?" Jack asked.

She looked around at the people she could see. "Oh, I don't know. It was pretty dark. Why would he be here?"

"He wouldn't," Jack said. "Don't worry about it. If you like, I can have someone come around and look, maybe watch your place for a night, in case he comes back."

The man beside Sharon spoke up. "I don't think that will be necessary," he said. "He left pretty quickly, and he didn't come back the next night. But there was one other funny thing."

Jack looked at the man, most likely the husband. "What's that?"

"The flood lights are supposed to come on if someone moves around in the yard. But they didn't. I checked them the next day, and he had unscrewed them. He could reach that high," the man said, holding his fingertips in the air. Jack raised his hand and pantomimed unscrewing a light bulb at that spot.

"Yeah, so he might have been as tall as you, almost," the man said.

"Could he have been wearing gloves?" Jack asked. "Do you think the bulbs had been on long enough to get hot?"

Sharon and the man looked at one another. "Maybe," Sharon said. "I didn't see his hands."

Jack took out two business cards. "If you think of anything else, give me a call," he said, and handed each of them a card.

He looked over at Worthington.

"Already on it," the man said. "I'm having someone sweep it for bugs this afternoon."

The rest of the morning was uneventful. Jack hated funerals, but he and Gonzales sat through all of the speakers and listened to the minister drone on about life, and tragedy, and how religion answered all of the hard questions. Jack had his doubts.

§

Jack and Gonzales had just entered the station when they heard a woman's voice, loud and angry, coming from a just-opened doorway.

"That is so typically male a reaction! Like he would have been faithful if he knew she had a gun! How about being faithful because she's his wife, for god's sake! Or was that in the pre-nup too?"

Jack turned the corner and faced the angry woman.

"Hello, Liz," he said.

His ex-wife turned towards him. When she saw who it was, she composed herself. "Hi, Jack," she said. "Nice group of guys you have here. You teach them everything they know?"

He shrugged. "They're cops. Can't teach them anything."

"The cops I can handle," she said. "It's the assistant DA that has your boss in a twist. I want that gun," she said. "Our people need to look at it before some jerk in the county lab erases evidence 'by accident' like they did in the MacMurtaugh case."

"Not my department," Jack said. "I only handle the ones where the bullets actually hit someone."

"Too bad she'd never used a gun before, the guy deserved it," she said.

"Wouldn't that make your job a little harder?" Jack asked.

"Oh, not at all," she said. "Then I'd be dealing with *you*. *You* I can handle in my sleep."

Jack smiled. "Not any more, I'm afraid," he said.

"Oh god," she sighed, "You *did* teach them everything they know." But she was smiling as she left the building.

Gonzales followed Jack back to his desk.

"Don't you miss that?" he said.

"What, bickering with my ex-wife?" Jack asked.

"No, the make-up sex. Man, everyone in the building has dreams of nailing your ex-wife."

"I thought that was just Sally in booking," Jack said.

"Admit it, Jack. You married her because she's hot."

"I married her despite the fact that she always woke up hung over. She never fell asleep, she always passed out. I thought I could help, be her protector. When we finally found a program

133

that worked, she found out she didn't need a protector anymore. And just for your information, no one looks hot puking in a commode at three a.m. after a party."

Gonzales held up his hands and leaned away from Jack. "Whoa, you've got issues there. Sounds like even you want to nail your ex-wife."

Jack relaxed and looked at his partner. "Well," he said. "She *is* hot."

Gonzales placed the two video cameras and their receivers on the desk. "Well, let's see who was at the party."

They spent the next two hours downloading snapshots and video and sorting through everything to make a collection of faces. Many of the images were blurred either by the motion of the cell phone cameras, or the motion of the subject, or simply by being too far away, but in the end, they had a decent face shot of everyone at the funeral.

They separated the photos into two groups by gender and tried to give names to all the male images they could. There were too many missing to draw any conclusions. *Was he even there?* Jack wondered.

Chapter 15: She hoped to finish in time; that was a lot to put in a suicide note.

The bus station had WiFi. Sandra read through her email while she waited for the bus to Long Beach. Jeff Worthington had uploaded the videos and had created stills of faces, each one labeled with the person's name, and in many cases, an image of their signature in the guest book.

He had labeled the faces of those he knew to be staff, and the two detectives. There were sixteen images with no labels, but Sandra identified four of them. She copied all of the stills into a new account at a photo-sharing site, using detective.jack.morgan @ gmail.com as the email address, and then found that the detective was online. At this time of the day, he'd be home already, and his computer should be on and connected, but she didn't know if he'd be at his computer.

She put on her headset, clicked to set up the video chat, and went back to reading her email while she waited for a response. There was a report from ClickBank that Xavier Hargrove had been sent a check for sales of his eBook. She smiled at that. It would not begin to cover what an average day was costing her, but it was a beginning.

Jack Morgan's face appeared in the video chat window.

Sandra pressed the mute button to speak.

"Hi there," she said. "I'm in a noisy place, so I'm going to mute my mike when I'm not speaking. How did it go at the funeral?" She clicked the mute button again. No sense letting him hear what was going on in the bus station and drawing conclusions.

"I'm still going through the photos," he said. "Nothing stands out yet."

"I have a dozen yet to identify myself," she said. "I emailed the whole lot to your new email address."

"Only a dozen? Either you work really fast, or we shot a lot more people than you did."

"Jeff's really good at what he does. Setting up the camera to watch people sign in really helps," Sandra said. She could hear him typing and imagined him logging into the email account.

"Smart move," Morgan said. "I'll have to remember that one."

135

"You guys have handwriting analysis people, right?" Sandra asked. "You can have them look at the signatures to see if they think someone is faking the name?"

"And you can match the person signing with a face. Wouldn't that be convenient," Morgan said.

"I doubt our guy would sign in," Sandra said. "But that helps too, since we can eliminate the signers from our list."

"If they're not faking the signature," Morgan said. Sandra could see light flickering on his face as he pulled up the images she had sent.

"It will take me a while to see if one of us caught someone the other didn't," he said.

"Take your time," she said. "I'm not going anywhere."

"Then why are you in a bus terminal?" Morgan asked.

"They have good WiFi," Sandra replied and remembered to mute the microphone this time.

"I can knock your dozen down to ten," Jack said. "Two of these guys are federal marshals."

"Which ones?" Sandra asked, pulling up the images on her screen.

"You have them labeled as 'tall suit' and 'chubby suit.' My boss calls them Stanley and Oliver."

Sandra smiled. "Your boss doesn't care for federal assistance, I take it. I have a friend doing pairwise analysis, to make an association network of all the people in the videos. When he's done, we'll have a list of who likely knows who, and we can see if there are any loners in the crowd. But also, we can ask people we know what the missing names are, since we'll know who knows whom."

"I learn new tricks every time I talk to you," Morgan said.

"How nice to be appreciated," Sandra said. "And speaking of which, thanks for working the Hilton thing. I've never had a guy risk taking a bullet for me." She suddenly got serious, and her voice wavered. "Except Scott. Crap."

Morgan said nothing. Sandra wiped away a tear, and her eye immediately filled with another.

"I think we can rule out Worthington," Morgan said.

136

Sandra sniffed and wiped her eyes again, smiling weakly. "That's what the crap about Oaxaca was all about?"

"Well, yes, but that's not what rules him out. He was at a convention in Chicago when Tremain was killed. Guest speaker."

"I'm sure he'll be happy to know he's not on your list," Sandra said. She looked at the photos of the two marshals. "Do these guys have real names?"

"Laurel and Hardy? You know, I don't think I ever got their names. I'll send you an email."

"Send it to yourself at the one I set up for you. That's why I said not to change the password. We can each write emails, but never actually send them, just read each other's drafts. They go over the network less that way."

"Ok, then, I'll draft an email with their names."

"Are these the guys who found Rafael and the bus?" Sandra asked.

"You heard about that, then. Is that why you're in a bus terminal?"

"They have lockers for all your stuff, so you don't have to lug it around," Sandra said.

"You're awfully quick with these evasions," Morgan said.

"You're not that slow yourself. We should team up when this is over. I could use someone with your access."

"I think they call that a conflict of interest," Morgan said.

"Au contraire, mon frère," she said. "It's an alignment of interests. Mutual back scratching society. You can clear it with your boss. Or your wife, if that's what you meant."

"I'm no longer married," he said.

"How'd I miss that? The Elizabeth Morgan in the news last week was your sister or something?"

"My ex-wife. She kept the name," Morgan said.

"I didn't mean to pry," Sandra said, sensing something in his voice. "Well, actually, I did, I mean, when I looked you up. Had to know what I was up against. Strictly professional."

"I understand."

"Touchy subject?" Sandra asked, softly.

"Not particularly."

"It just sounded a little like she kept the house and the dog as well as the name," Sandra said.

"She would have stuck me with the dog," Morgan said. "But yes, she got the house. I couldn't have made the mortgage anyway."

"Ouch! Sounds like a nice house."

"Her idea. I like simple," Morgan said.

"You've seen my place. Show me around," Sandra said.

Morgan hesitated. "You want to see this place?"

"Hey big boy," Sandra said, lowering her voice to try to sound sexy. "I showed you mine..."

There was a pause, and then the image shook as Morgan picked up the computer. "This is the kitchen table," he said. "And the remains of Chinese take-out."

"Hold it still," Sandra said. The image settled, and she could see a small table and two open boxes of take-out. The rest of the table was covered with files and papers.

"I like a man who can handle chopsticks," she said, noting the lack of silverware.

"I like a meal that doesn't involve washing dishes," Morgan said.

"Touché," Sandra said. "What else ya got?"

The image moved again. "Kitchen sink."

"Empty, as promised," she said.

The image blurred and then settled. "Bedroom."

"A bachelor who actually makes the bed," Sandra said.

"You never know when some nice lady on the Internet will demand a walk-through," Morgan replied.

"Indeed. Or when some nice lady in a bar wants to follow you home."

"I've given up picking up drunks," Morgan said.

"There you go, something else we have in common."

The scene went into motion again as Morgan walked into another room. "Living room," he said.

"That's a big TV," Sandra said. "Compensating for something?"

"She upgraded," Morgan said. "This used to be in the gym."

138

"Better than getting stuck with a dog?"

"Don't have to walk it."

Sandra noticed movement around her. "Thanks for the tour," she said. "I have to go."

"Have a nice trip," Morgan said.

She disconnected before the loudspeaker announced the bus to Long Beach.

§

On the bus, she sat in the far back, her computer in her lap. She did not want anyone to see what she was working on. She had a feeling now that she could trust Jack Morgan to do what was needed. But rather than trust that he would know what to do in any situation, she wanted to try to construct as many scenarios as she could think of, and plan contingencies for each. Since her life would depend on this going just right, she wanted to be sure. She hoped to finish in time; that was a lot to put in what might end up being a suicide note.

But the planning was not the only thing that had to be done. As the bus bounced through the desert, Sandra used the on-board WiFi to make sure Balrog had finished the association network and sent it to Morgan. He had not found a lone wolf, but there were still some people yet to identify. It bothered her than none of the ones remaining looked likely to have been capable of overcoming Scott Tremain. If the killer had been monitoring the funeral, he may have used one of them as a proxy. Jeff Worthington had found no cameras or bugs other than his and the ones he had loaned the detectives. But most of the people there had cell phones.

One other hope she had rested in finding a cell phone that correlated with locations she suspected the killer frequented. She had found him this way once before, but those phones had been ditched when the disk became public. She had JersyGrrl's computers working on that, correlating all the cell phone traffic from the funeral, locations in Sacramento, the police department, and Sharon Tremain's house at the times she thought he might have been at those places. Even with tens of thousands of computers at her disposal, the amount of data was large, and the size of the problem was even larger. And the way the cell phone traffic was collected, she could not be sure that something wasn't missed. But actually hacking into the phone company was not in her skill set. Inserting supposedly secure routers in between phone company data centers was as close as she could get. And as those got found and disabled, her network of data feeds was shrinking. And if the killer never used the same phone twice, she was just out of luck, unless there was a clear pattern in who they called.

140

A possible flaw in her plans was that the killer might not be watching the hospice where Sandra's mother was staying. Sandra knew that a place like that was the best way to find her, and if she was doing the search, she would definitely have the place under surveillance. But was the killer smart enough, and did he have the resources? She'd have to make sure the word of her presence in Long Beach got out in more than one way, and yet remained credible.

She was tired. More than once, she leaned back and closed her eyes for a moment, lowering the screen on her computer in case she fell asleep. But tired as she was, problem after problem presented itself, and she covered each contingency with another note in the computer.

Would bus stations be watched? Get off in Pasadena and take a cab to Long Beach. Once word was out that she was visiting her mother, how soon would the federal marshals get there? If they arrived before she knew who the killer was, that could be fatal. It's very hard to hide in jail.

She awoke when the bus lurched to a stop. Barstow. She looked down at her computer and decided she needed to send the file to Morgan before she ran out of battery power. If she thought of any more problems, she could send an addendum.

Late at night at the Barstow bus stop, there was not a lot to see. She and a few other passengers took the opportunity to stretch their legs. She walked and stretched, and thought about the plan. She was in uncharted territory, having never operated in this fashion before. She was always the lurker in the shadows, the spy from afar, the moth around the flame of the target. Now she was to be the flame, to draw the moth to her. No longer hidden in the shadows, she was about to become the bright light. Dangerous business. She would need everyone's help.

People started filing back onto the bus, and Sandra found her seat at the back again. She stretched out as best she could on the seat and was asleep in a few minutes. She did not wake until the bus had already gone over the pass and was descending into the valley towards Ontario. The sky outside was beginning to lighten, and dawn was less than an hour away. She opened the laptop and connected to the net.

Balrog had left her an email. All it said was "Good news." But the icon by his name said he was online, and she clicked on it to start a chat session. His face showed up on the screen after only a few seconds. She could see sunlight behind him. He was on east coast time, by the angle of the shadow.

"Hey girl, you look like shit," he said.

"Why thank you," she replied. "Shall I cut the video?"

"No, I'm just saying you might want to comb your hair or something."

"I just woke up on the bus," Sandra said. "At least I think I'm awake. What's the good news?"

"Well, the botnet narrowed the phone list down to 483 possibles, and I thought that was a small enough data set to start playing around. I ran some correlations, and two of the numbers pop out. I think your secret admirer is twins."

Sandra let that sink in. "That doesn't fit the other data," she said. "This guy's a loner. If someone knows who he is, they end up dead. None of his other numbers have ever linked to another burner phone."

"It popped right out," Balrog said. "Two phones, calling each other at the same cell towers, at the funeral, and in Sacramento, and in San Jose. And last night in Las Vegas."

"Where in Vegas?"

"Bellagio. Probably adjoining rooms."

"But not Henderson?"

"Can't tell where they are when they aren't on the phone. We can't track like the cops can."

"He's smart enough to remove the battery anyway," she said.

"But not smart enough to ditch the phones after each call? What's up with that?"

"He has someone on the inside at the phone company. That's what tripped up Jackson Hardy. He thought he could tell whenever a trace was logged on a number. He didn't think there were other ways to track a cell phone."

"So, what, he's leaving a trail to act as bait? Find out who is tracing him, and track you down that way?"

"Sounds pretty remote. But we can play with it anyway, in addition to what I've already got going. I'll ask Jack to trace the numbers, and make it look like the request came from Long Beach. He's probably already on a plane there by now anyway, if he's read his email."

"You're being pretty trusting of a cop. Isn't he supposed to arrest you as soon as he sees you?"

"We all want the same thing. We just go about it differently. But the plan is that he won't see me until after he's arrested the bad guy. After that, he can throw me in jail, and I'll work on explaining everything to a judge and the D.A."

"I can tell you've never been in jail. Best get your explaining done ahead of time and avoid that hotel altogether," Balrog said.

"Good advice, I'm sure. But right now, I'm going to try to get another nap in before the bus gets to Long Beach."

Balrog smiled and made a small salute, and the screen went blank. Sandra closed the laptop and stretched back out on the uncomfortable seat. She drifted in and out of sleep as the bus crept into traffic.

Chapter 16: Self-defense was probably not an option in the wood chipper incident.

Chopsticks in his left hand, Jack used his right to bring up the photo gallery. The laptop shared the kitchen table with the takeout boxes, a tall stack of napkins, and a beer bottle that had just begun to sweat. He and Gonzales had spent the day sorting and labeling photos, but there was still a lot left to do. He hoped Gonzales had something better to do with his evening. For Jack, a beer, some egg rolls, and a homicide puzzle were the ingredients of a relaxing night.

The beer was finished, and he was about to get up and get a second one when the computer beeped and invited him to a video chat. He clicked on the OK button, and Millbarque's face appeared, lit from the screen of her laptop. There was institutional fluorescent lighting behind her and rows of airport seats. The sounds of a busy terminal suddenly burst from the laptop speakers as she clicked on a button.

"Hi there. I'm in a busy place, so I'm going to mute my mike when I'm not speaking. How did it go at the funeral?" The sound clicked off, and Jack's kitchen was once again silent.

"I'm still going through the photos," Jack said. He tried to pick out what was wrong with the airport. Millbarque spoke, and he listened to the noise behind her voice, trying to pick out what the problem was. Then he figured it out.

"Take your time," Millbarque was saying. "I'm not going anywhere."

"Then why are you in a bus terminal?" Jack asked.

"They have good WiFi," she answered, not pausing. The sound clicked off again.

They talked for a while. She got emotional when she remembered her partner, and Jack felt a familiar protective urge as she became more human, no longer the computer genius that was always a step ahead. He changed the subject.

"I think we can rule out Worthington," he said. Her smile told him it was working. They got back to business, and she was once again the girl with the quick evasions, the spark in her eye that told you she was one move ahead of you.

144

"Or your wife," she was saying. "If that's what you meant."

"I'm no longer married," he said.

"How'd I miss that?" she said. Jack listened to her voice, but her eyes had changed. He'd have to replay the video later to be sure, but it looked like her eyes got just a little bit wider, as if something was suddenly a lot more interesting. Or maybe he was just wishing they had.

"Ouch! Sounds like a nice house," she said.

"Her idea. I like simple," Jack answered.

"You've seen my place. Show me around." Jack realized she meant for him to aim the camera around his room. He looked around quickly and was surprised that the place was actually presentable. He had not been spending a lot of time at home lately. He picked up the computer and aimed the camera down at the table.

"I like a man who can handle chopsticks," she said.

He moved the camera to the kitchen and hesitated a moment before walking into the bedroom. Had he left anything embarrassing out in plain view? But the room was neat, the bed made as usual, and he moved into the living room.

She commented on the big-screen TV then seemed to be all business.

"Thanks for the tour," she said. "I have to go."

"Have a nice trip," Jack said and watched the screen go blank. She was on the move again and did not seem happy about it.

During the conversation, he had logged in to the new email account she had set up for him. He had only looked at the dozen unknowns, but now he looked over the rest of what was there. The photo sharing service had a very neatly arranged gallery of photos, most with names associated with them, and short video clips of them signing into the funeral guest book. He started matching up the names to the photos he and Gonzales had taken. Worthington hadn't missed anyone.

It was a little after midnight when the computer beeped again, this time with new email in the shared account. Jack opened it up, and it was a diagram made of little boxes with a face and a name in each one, and arrows linking them, each with an annotation, such as "works for," "sister of," and so on. Most of them simply said "calls" or "is called by."

At the bottom of the page, one line said, "No lone wolves." That phrasing brought back a memory. An old case. They had been looking for a lone gunman, who they had all come to call the lone wolf. The case had been intractable until they finally realized the man had a partner. Jack went back to the diagram and began marking all of the links where pairs of people had no ties to others at the funeral. Nothing popped out. It was late. Sleep on it, and maybe it will make more sense in the morning. He shut the laptop, put the takeout containers in the trash, and went to bed. Tired as he was, sleep did not come quickly. Something was nagging at the back of his brain.

§

In the morning, back at the police station, Jack could hear loud voices as he walked in.

"Can you believe that?" Chief Wilson was shouting down the hallway. "He's claiming self-defense. It was a fucking wood chipper for chrissake! A wood chipper. A jury of monkeys wouldn't believe that was self defense!"

Gonzales was already at his desk. He seemed happy about something.

"I told her," he said as Jack approached.

"What's that?" Jack asked.

"I told Vicky about the Hilton thing. Everybody with their guns out. My partner almost getting shot. She was cool. Asked me how many times in my career I had someone point a gun at me."

"What did you say?" Jack asked.

"I said never, which is the truth. Not even that day."

"And then?"

"Then she says police work isn't as dangerous as people think it is. She already looked it all up, when we started dating. She said garbage men and truck drivers have more fatalities. Farmers almost twice as many, and fishing is like five times as dangerous."

"You got laid," Jack said.

"Well, yeah. Then she said she was leaving me for a fisherman with a big insurance policy."

Jack placed his computer down on the desk. "Millbarque's on the move. Something is up."

"You talked to her last night?"

"She was at a bus terminal. One with regular service to Phoenix and San Diego," Jack said.

"What's there for her?"

"I think she's going to Long Beach."

"Something wrong with her mom? I mean, something new?" Gonzales asked.

"I don't know yet. The woman running the hospice promised to call if anything came up, or if Millbarque showed. Said the marshals asked for the same service. But I haven't gotten any calls."

"We check anyway, right?"

"Damn right. A bus from Las Vegas would be there by now."
Jack opened the laptop and connected to the web to look up bus
schedules. When he was logged in, he had email waiting from
Millbarque. He opened it.

"Shit," he said, looking up at Gonzales. "She's got his cell
phone number. Numbers. There are two guys. Last calls were from
Vegas. She wants us to trace them, but to do it from Long Beach."

"What the hell?" Gonzales looked puzzled.

"She's setting herself up as bait," Jack said. He picked up the
phone. "Sally," he said into it. "I need two tickets to Long Beach,
California, as soon as possible. And get me the number of the local
police there, I'm going to need their help."

"I get to fly this time?" Gonzales asked.

"We may be springing for the tab ourselves," Jack said. "I'm
not sure Wilson is ready to pony up for another ticket this soon
after Sacramento."

Jack continued reading the email from Milbarque. "God damn,
she's got the whole thing mapped out like an NFL playbook."

He picked up the phone again and punched the same number.
"Sally, once I'm on the flight, phone the marshals' office to tell
them where I am. But not until I'm on the flight, OK?"

"Why bother?" Gonzales asked.

"It's on her list. But check this out," he said, pushing the
computer towards Gonzales and pointing at item seven.

"No sirens after the 911 call," Gonzales read aloud. "What's
that about?"

"If she calls the cavalry, she doesn't want to spook the perp.
This is really bad. It looks to me like she really is planning on
letting him get right up next to her."

Jack pulled the computer back in front of him, and studied the
screen. "Jaime, get the phone trace people on the line and call
Worthington. What do you want to bet he's in Long Beach right
now?"

Chapter 17: What if he was already dead when I shot him?

"How many garbage men are there in California?"

"Really? You're in this place, at this time, and you want to play the game?"

"Your sister won't play it with me."

Sandra sat down on the chair next to her mother's hospital bed.

"All right. 'How on earth do I know that?'" She paused for a moment. "They work eight hour shifts five days a week, I'll assume. And maybe it takes a full minute on average to process a house, counting breaks and lunch. California has 30 some million people --"

"Thirty-seven," her mother interrupted.

"Not a significant difference to the calculation." Sandra tried not to look at her watch.

"But you knew better."

"Most people find unnecessary precision an annoyance in conversation. I was being polite out of reflex and forgot who I was talking to."

"Ouch," her mother said.

"Figure four people per house, so there's 8 million houses to do each week. Forty hours is 240 minutes, so one guy can do 240 houses in his week. Eight million divided by 240 is how many garbage men there are in California, to one significant digit."

"You're not going to do the arithmetic?"

"A million divided by thirty?"

"Does thirty-three thousand seem a little small to you?"

"I can look it up for you in a minute if you want to change the rules."

"Goodness no. I got the same number, it just seemed a little low."

"Which direction did you come from?"

"I read that Waste Management had 45,000 employees in North America."

"Meaning half of them are collectors."

"You're skipping some steps there."

"Game's over, I don't have to show my work anymore. Especially to someone who already did it."

Her mother looked at her in silence for just a moment.

"Is something bothering you, dear?"

Sandra slumped back in the chair and put her hands up. "Mom, you're in hospice. I didn't think I'd get here in time. Something really bad has happened, and it's taken me days to get here when I should have been here all along, and you act like nothing has happened."

"You want me to act like I'm dying?" her mother said softly, a smile on her face.

"No, you're acting beautifully," Sandra said sniffing, tears wetting her lips. "You're just perfect."

"So are you, dear. Now, it's your turn."

"Oh, give me a minute! I haven't played Fermi Questions in years, and this is the hard part. They said you gave them a scare last night."

"They just don't like people playing with their fancy equipment."

"They thought you had died."

"So they sent someone in to check. See, they expect the equipment to malfunction. They wouldn't have jobs if kindly people like me didn't give them something to do."

"These people aren't your toys, mother. They care about the people they help."

"What good is dying if you can't have fun? I'll be out of their hair soon enough."

Sandra ignored the tears blinking on the rims of her lashes.

"How many street names does my GPS know?"

Her mother grinned broadly. "'Oh, my goodness. 'How on earth do I know that?'" she said as if talking to a young child.

Now Sandra could look at her watch.

"I happen to know there are about eight million miles of road in the U.S.," her mother said. "But I don't think you knew that, so I'm trying to figure out how you got to the answer I did. I figure on average a road goes one or two miles before meeting another one, counting all the long stretches of rural highway and all the crowded city streets. I figure four to eight million street names. How did you get there?"

"I looked at how much memory the GPS had," Sandra said. "I came up with six million."

"We both cheated," her mother said. "Not the best Fermi Question. Your sister wouldn't have had a chance."

"I said I was rusty. And I've got other things on my mind."

"Sometimes the point of the game is to get those other things off your mind," her mother said. "Do you want to talk about your troubles instead?"

"Mom, I know damn well why you took apart the morphine drip machine," Sandra said.

"I thought we were going to talk about *your* troubles," her mother said. "Your sister wouldn't tell me anything. But we both know only the worst trouble would have kept you from being here."

"Someone murdered my business partner. The police are looking for *me*. But I think he's after me too, and he's using the police to find me."

"But you came to see your mother anyway."

"It's part of the plan. Get him out in the open, at a place of my choosing."

"I'm one of your two birds," her mother said.

"You're always my first bird," Sandra said. "But the second bird won't know what hit him."

§

The perimeter alarm sounded, loudly enough to be heard anywhere in the apartment but not so shrill as to jangle nerves. Sandra was relieved. The waiting was over. Now she could just be scared to death.

She walked to the computer monitor on the table, strategically arranged with a view of the door, and big metal filing cabinets to duck behind if something went wrong. She sat down and watched on the monitor as the man approach the door. He was tall and slender, but carried himself like an athlete. He crouched in front of the door, and Sandra could hear the clicks and scrapes of lock-picking equipment in use. She smiled. It takes longer to pick a lock when it isn't locked. He had not even tried the door. She looked at the countdown timer on the computer monitor. Six minutes was a long time.

The door opened slowly, just enough for the man to slip in. He turned and quietly closed the door behind him, not seeing Sandra in the shadows. He had a gun in one hand, and a huge hunting knife in the other.

"That's far enough," Sandra said quietly. The man spun around to face her. The gun was aimed at her chest.

"You don't want to touch that trip wire," Sandra said, pointing towards his feet. She moved her finger slowly across the room, showing how the wire ran from the wall behind the door, and over to a fire extinguisher bolted to the far wall. "When you fill a fire extinguisher with propane, it makes a hell of a flame thrower," she said. The nozzle of the fire extinguisher pointed directly at the man holding the gun.

"I could just shoot you from here," the man said.

"Which is why you brought the big intimidating knife," Sandra said. "But apparently you've never seen a deadman switch before. If I let go of this," she said, holding up a small black box, "Those propane tanks detonate, and the entire building goes up."

He looked around the room. There were half a dozen tanks of propane, wired together with boxes duct-taped to their sides. He seemed to be thinking for a long time.

"I take it killing Scott Tremain was a little easier for you," Sandra said. "Why the knife this time? Tired of the wire garrote?"

The man looked at the knife and smiled. "You think you have it all figured out?" he said.

"I figured you came here to talk," Sandra said. "And then kill me. I rather object to that last part, but we're both here, and I'm in the mood for a conversation. What did you come here to find out?"

The man started to step over the trip wire.

"You really don't want to do that," Sandra said. "I can pull the wire from here if I like. This place is insured. I'll lose my cleaning deposit, but that's a risk I'll take."

He put his foot back down.

"So ask away," Sandra said. "What would you like to know?"

"Who's your inside guy?" the man asked.

"Inside what?" Sandra asked back.

"Inside WITSEC," the man said. "Who gives you the new IDs of the witnesses?"

"There is no inside man," Sandra said.

"Bullshit," the man said. "There's no way you could find them without someone on the inside. I know. I'm on the inside. I know how the system works."

"And I know how the system fails," Sandra said. "You can't beat raw math and statistics. With enough data and good correlations, there are no secrets."

"That's horseshit. Give up your inside man, this will be a lot less painful. The gumshoe was stupid too, thought it was worth hours of pain. He died anyway. What's this guy to you? I found you. I found the gumshoe. I'll find him eventually. Give him up."

"So you can kill me and get on with your life? Hardly an incentive. But indulge me. You're a federal marshal. What made you sell out? Why kill the witnesses you're sworn to protect?"

"Are you kidding?" the man said. "They're all scumbags. Criminals, drug dealers, thugs, low lifes. They turn on their slimeball friends the moment things get tight, and they hide in WITSEC and get new lives. They're scum. I arrange for the other scum to clean up the mess, in exchange for a very nice paycheck. I'm an entrepreneur. Doing what the marshals should have been doing."

"How noble of you. What about your friends in the marshals service who got killed along the way?"

"Collateral damage. I don't need putzes like that as friends. They have no imagination. No drive."

"Not like you," Sandra said. She looked at the countdown timer. Three minutes. This was harder than she had imagined.

The man started walking towards the fire extinguisher. "I've been wondering," he said. "Why you don't just pull the wire."

"Another step and I will," Sandra said.

"I don't think so," the man said, and he reached the extinguisher. He grabbed the nozzle and aimed it at Sandra.

"You're still forgetting the deadman switch," Sandra said.

"I'll bet you scream a whole lot before you actually decide to kill yourself," the man said, raising the knife and stepping over the trip wire. He took a step towards Sandra.

There was a bang and a sizzle, and the man fell to his knees, dropping the knife and the gun. Sandra jumped up and grabbed the gun as the man writhed in pain on the floor.

"God damn it, Jeff, you're supposed to wait for the SWAT team!" Sandra said. "You could have been killed."

Jeff Worthington stepped out of the shadowed hallway into the room, the Taser in his hand trailing wires to the darts in the marshal's back.

"It looked like things were about to go badly," Worthington said.

"What if you had missed?" she asked.

"I have another shot," he said.

Sandra ejected the magazine from the gun and examined the bullets. "So this is what those expensive bullets look like," she said, sliding the magazine back in with a firm click, and flicking the safety off. The man on the floor had stopped writhing.

"Two and a half minutes," Sandra said, looking at the computer monitor again. "Then we turn him over to SWAT, and the whole problem goes away."

The marshal looked up, then grabbed the knife and jumped to his feet, swinging the knife at Worthington. The gun in Sandra's hand made a deafening sound in the small room, and the back of the marshal's head exploded onto the far wall.

"God damn this thing kicks," Sandra said. "I was *not* aiming at his head."

"He was attacking us," Worthington said. "Clearly self defense. All the cameras will show that."

Sandra looked up at the cameras placed around the room, recording everything to remote computers. The room seemed extremely quiet after the deafening gunshot. There was a click behind the door.

"Len?" a voice said from behind the door. "I thought you were going to use the knife."

Sandra motioned Worthington back into the hallway. He disappeared into the shadows. Sandra sat down in the chair, resting the gun on the table to control it better.

The door opened slowly and a hand appeared, holding a gun. *This guy really is an idiot,* Sandra thought, and aimed the gun at the back of his hand, and pulled the trigger. Even when she was expecting the loud explosion, it was still an amazing shock. There was a scream from the door as the gun slammed against the wall, followed closely by two severed fingers. The fat marshal fell against the door, opening it wide, holding his maimed hand and screaming. There was another pop and sizzle, and the fat man dropped to the floor and twitched as the Taser brought him down.

Worthington stepped into the room and retrieved the gun, holding the bloody object between his thumb and forefinger, and carrying it to the table.

Bright lights lit up the room as headlights streamed in through the open door.

"They're 42 seconds late," Sandra said.

Chapter 18: His final thought was what a good deal he had gotten on the parachute.

Jack Morgan hated the waiting. Millbarque had deliberately not shared the location with anyone, saying she would call 911 when the killer showed up. However, she had some confidence that the response time would be six minutes from the police station. Jack was wearing a wireless earpiece so he could monitor the call when it came in. The dispatcher would patch him in automatically. In the meantime, he waited, listening with one ear to the chatter of the police station, and the story his new friend was telling. The story was somewhat disjointed, as the man was typing in an unrelated police report as he spoke.

Gonzales had chosen to ride with a patrol car, figuring he had an even chance of being closer to Millbarque than the station was when the call came in. Jack knew it was because Gonzales hated waiting even more than he did.

"So the guy's last thought was what a great deal he got on the parachute," the man said, finishing his story.

Jack looked up, distracted. He smiled, as if he had found the ending as humorous as his companion had. "I wonder how you'd know," he said.

"Know what?"

"What his final thoughts were. Like maybe he was talking to someone on his cell phone as he was falling. Or taking notes or something."

"Me, I'd be screaming my head off. I hate heights," the man said, finishing the report with a finger stabbing the Enter key with much more force than necessary.

Jack jumped when the phone in his hand rang, and he quickly fumbled to take the call. "…it makes a hell of a flame thrower," he heard in his ear, the 911 call already several seconds in progress. The man at the desk was already on his feet, and another pair of officers hurried after them out to the cars.

"No sirens," Jack reminded them and jumped into the passenger seat. The car lurched quickly out into the street, lights flashing, driving as often in the turn lane as in normal traffic lanes. There were far too many cars on the road. Without sirens, this might take longer than six minutes. Jack looked at the navigation display, trying to get a feel for the distance without interfering with the driver's attention.

"Why the knife this time? Tired of the wire garrote?" Jack heard in his ear. His right foot pushed a non-existent accelerator pedal into the floor. The car swerved into another lane and passed a slow-moving SUV.

"The gumshoe was stupid too, thought it was worth hours of pain. He died anyway." Jack could barely hear the words in his ear, between the traffic noise and the inherent faintness due to the distance the man must be from the microphone.

"The guy just admitted to killing Scott Tremain," Jack said to the driver. "He definitely thinks he's going to kill her tonight. Whatever she has going, he isn't afraid of it. I don't think we have a lot of time."

"Roger that," the man said, swerving past another car. "Your buddy's going to beat us there. SWAT is a minute behind, maybe two."

Jack listened to the phone. "You're a federal marshal. What made you sell out?"

"God damn!" he shouted. "It's Laurel and Hardy!"

"What?" the driver asked.

"The two federal marshals from the WITSEC program. They are the ones killing witnesses."

The car turned a corner hard. Someone honked. "Another step and I will," Jack heard in his ear.

The radio belched, and Jack heard Gonzales' voice. "We're about three minutes out." No codes, no police jargon, just Gonzales, breaking radio silence in a way he thought might not alert an eavesdropper.

"I'll bet you scream a whole lot before you actually decide to kill yourself," Jack heard in his ear. Three minutes was not going to be fast enough.

157

"God damn it, Jeff, you're supposed to wait for the SWAT team!" Jack had no trouble hearing this time, the shout in his ear leaving it ringing. The car flew over a dip in the road, and Jack's seat belt barely kept his head from hitting the ceiling.

"Something's happened," Jack said to the driver. "Sounds like they're talking about him getting shot, but I didn't hear any gunfire."

"Two and a half minutes," Jack heard in his ear. The car took another corner, tires squealing and losing traction for a moment. Something exploded in Jack's ear, and he yanked the earpiece away with a shout.

"I heard that from over here," the driver said.

Jack fumbled to put the earpiece back. "I was *not* aiming at his head," he heard Sandra say.

"She's still talking," Jack said to the driver. "Sounds like she fired at the marshal." He reached for the radio microphone.

"Gunfire at destination, friendlies are armed."

"Roger that," came Gonzales' voice.

The car swerved past another slow sedan. Jack thought it might be OK to use the sirens now but hesitated. Then there was another explosion in his ear.

"God damn!" Jack said.

"What the hell's going on?" the driver asked.

"Can't tell. There's a bunch of yelling, but no words. Man's voice. I can't tell if Millbarque is OK. I don't hear her voice."

"We're at the scene," Gonzales said.

"Be careful, there was another gunshot," Jack said. "I can't tell if she's OK."

"Gonzales is going around the back," came an unfamiliar voice on the radio. "I have lights on the front door. It's open. Some movement on the floor. Waiting for backup."

The car turned the final corner, and Jack could see the police cruiser, all its lights on, sitting half on the sidewalk in a driveway. They pulled up next to it, adding their lights to the scene. Jack jumped out.

"Millbarque!" he shouted. "You OK?"

158

"We're OK," came a woman's voice. "Come on in. But don't step in all the blood, it's a mess in here."

The fat marshal was on the floor, still writhing in a pool of blood, holding his right hand and whimpering. Millbarque and Worthington were standing over him, both with their hands up in the air.

"You can put your hands down," Jack said. "What happened here?"

"It's all on video," Sandra said. "From five different angles. When the big guy came at me with a knife and a gun, Jeff Tased him. I picked up the gun, but I forgot about the knife. The guy recovered, grabbed the knife, and took a swing at Jeff. I shot him."

"Then the other guy came in," Jeff said.

"Actually, only his hand came in, holding a gun," Sandra said. "I shot the gun out of his hand before he could see me."

Gonzales was behind the two, having come in through the back door. "Christ on a pogo stick," he said, surveying the room. He spoke into the radio he was holding. "We need an ambulance and a coroner," he said.

Four men in flak jackets labeled SWAT rushed into the room, and spread out through the house. "Bomb squad!" one of them yelled, seeing the tanks and wires.

"Those are just fakes," Sandra said. "They're helium tanks from a party store, with some duct tape and wire. We couldn't find any propane tanks in a hurry, so we taped over the labels."

Jack looked at her for a while in silence as the rest of the room bustled busily around them. "You are one gutsy lady," he said.

"Who, me?" she replied.

§

It was a long night writing up the reports. Sandra and Worthington had provided the video of the entire evening's events, and the whole station was watching from any of five different viewpoints. Transcripts were made of everything said, and evidence was collected and logged. Sandra was on the phone with her sister.

"I thought about not telling you," she said. "But I just couldn't do that to you. But she clearly wants to choose her own time." There was a pause as she listened to the phone. Jack tried to look busy with something else as he listened in.

"She won't want us there when she does it. If she's alone, then no one can be accused of assisting." She listened again.

"You want to come down here to the station? I'll probably be here all night." She listened again.

"I'd guess tonight. I called her to tell her my problems were over. I think she was waiting for that. Give her a call, let her tell you in her own way." Another pause.

"Ok. I'll see you in an hour or two. No rush. I may be spending some time as a guest of the city. They haven't let me know yet." She listened.

"Sis, I just killed a guy and maimed another. Federal marshals. I may get anything from jail time to an award and keys to the city. But the gears have to turn for a while."

Jack waited a polite minute after she disconnected. "Accused of assisting?" he said.

Sandra looked up at him. He seemed concerned about her.

"It's too bad you won't get to meet my mother," she said, trying to keep her voice steady. "She's an amazing woman."

She paused to compose herself. "You know how people joke about taking things apart, and having pieces left over when they put it back together? When mom took something apart, and that was all the time, if there were pieces left over, they were the pieces that were slowing it down." She took a deep breath. "Whenever we would go to a motel, she would take apart the shower head. Inside almost all of them is a little plastic washer called a flow restrictor. Its job is to keep people from wasting water. But it keeps the water pressure too low. They have them in kitchen faucets, too, and it takes forever to fill a teapot. Not in our house."

"Mom took apart the little gadget by her bed that lets her dial up the amount of morphine she needs. I'm sure they have some little gadget in there that prevents overdoses. But since a morphine overdose can be treated if it's caught in time, she also took apart

160

the gadget that reports her vital signs and rings alarms. She had it all back together when they rushed into her room, but I'm sure there's a new feature now, where the alarms don't work.

"Mom likes to be in control. She wants to die on her own schedule, with dignity. Once Jen tells her she's OK with that, she'll probably do it as soon as the phone is back on the hook."

Jack looked into her eyes. "I don't know what to say."

"Just be there when I start crying. Just knowing you were there working the case helped me keep it together. But at some point I'm going to have to lose it, and I'll really need a friend then."

Jack put his hand on the desk, palm up, and she took it in hers. Neither one spoke.